I0599072

# BAD BRIDESMAID

## BILLIONAIRES CLUB #11

### ELISE FABER

BAD BRIDESMAID
BY ELISE FABER
Newsletter sign-up

This is a work of fiction. Names, places, characters, and events are fictitious in every regard. Any similarities to actual events and persons, living or dead, are purely coincidental. Any trademarks, service marks, product names, or named features are assumed to be the property of their respective owners, and are used only for reference. There is no implied endorsement if any of these terms are used. Except for review purposes, the reproduction of this book in whole or part, electronically or mechanically, constitutes a copyright violation.

BAD BRIDESMAID
Copyright © 2021 Elise Faber
Print ISBN-13: 978-1-946140-96-8
Ebook ISBN-13: 978-1-946140-95-1
Cover Art by Jena Brignola

## BILLIONAIRE'S CLUB

Bad Night Stand

Bad Breakup

Bad Husband

Bad Hookup

Bad Divorce

Bad Fiancé

Bad Boyfriend

Bad Blind Date

Bad Wedding

Bad Engagement

Bad Bridesmaid

Bad Swipe

# BILLIONAIRE'S CLUB CAST OF CHARACTERS

Heroes and Heroines:

*Abigail Roberts (Bad Night Stand)* — founding member of the Sextant, hates wine, loves crocheting

*Jordan O'Keith (Bad Night Stand)* — Heather's brother, former owner of RoboTech

*Cecilia (CeCe) Thiele (Bad Breakup)* — former nanny to Hunter, talented artist

*Colin McGregor (Bad Breakup)* — Scottish duke, owner of McGregor Enterprises

*Heather O'Keith (Bad Husband)* — CEO of RoboTech, Jordan's sister

*Clay Steele (Bad Husband)* — Heather's business rival, CEO of Steele Technologies

*Kay (Bad Date)* — romance writer, hates to be stood up

*Garret Williams (Bad Date)* — former rugby player

*Rachel Morris (Bad Hookup)* — Heather's assistant, super-powers include being ultra-organized

*Sebastian (Bas) Scott (Bad Hookup)* — Devon Scott's brother, Clay's assistant

*Rebecca (Bec) Darden (Bad Divorce)* — kickass lawyer, New York roots

*Luke Pearson (Bad Divorce)* — Southern gentleman, CEO Pearson Energies

*Seraphina Delgado (Bad Fiancé)* — romantic to the core, looks like a bombshell, but even prettier on the inside

*Tate Connor (Bad Fiancé)* — tech genius, scared to be burned by love

*Lorelai (Bad Text)* — drunk texts don't make her happy

*Logan Smith (Bad Text)* — former military, sometimes drunk texts are for the best

*Kelsey Scott (Bad Boyfriend)* — Bas and Devon's sister, engineer at RoboTech, brilliant

*Tanner Pearson (Bad Boyfriend)* — Bas and Devon's childhood friend, photographer

*Trix Donovan (Bad Blind Date)* — Heather's sister, Jordan's half-sister, nurse who worked in war zones, poverty-stricken areas, and abroad for almost a decade

*Jet Hansen (Bad Blind Date)* — a doctor Trix worked with

*Molly Miller (Bad Wedding)* — owner of Molly's, a kickass bakery in San Francisco

*Jackson Davis (Bad Wedding)* — Molly's ex-fiancé

*Kate McLeod (Bad Engagement)* — Kelsey's college friend, advertiser extraordinaire, loves purple and Hermione Granger

*Jaime Huntingon (Bad Engagement)* — vet, does excellent man-bun

Heidi Greene (Bad Bridesmaid) — science, organization, and *Twilight* nerd

Brad Huntington (Bad Bridesmaid) — travel junkie, dreamy hazel eyes, hidden sweet side

Additional Characters:

*George O'Keith* — Jordan's dad
*Hunter O'Keith* — Jordan's nephew
*Bridget McGregor* — Colin's mom
*Lena McGregor* — Colin's sister
*Bobby Donovan* — Heather's half and Trix's full brother
*Frances and Sugar Delgado* — Sera's parents
*Devon Scott* — Kels and Bas's brother
*Becca Scott* — Kels and Bas's sister in law
*Heidi Greene* — Kels' friend since college
*Cora Hutchins* — Kels' friend since childhood

# ONE

Heidi

SHE WAS WEARING a bridesmaid's dress and holding a leash.

Not the strangest sentence ever uttered.

Unless, perhaps, she included what was on the other end of the leash.

Because she'd been escorted down the aisle by a rooster name Sir Fuzzy McFeatherston, or the Fuzz, for short.

He was cute. He was cocky—*ha*—and he was not happy to be on a leash.

Thankfully, though, the ceremony was wrapping up. The bride and groom—her best friend, Kate, and her almost-husband, Jaime—were kissing. Soon, she'd be able to put the rooster in the cage, and she could get to drinking.

Because her best friend was getting married.

After an engagement she had promised Heidi would be extremely long but had ended up sort of average because Kate hadn't been able to wait to make Jaime officially hers.

Barf.

Heidi loved Kate, loved Jaime, and how he treated Kate.

But she was losing her best friend.

So, yeah, maybe she was feeling a little mopey, but she wasn't going to let her funk ruin her friend's night. She was going to be the best rooster-wrangling bridesmaid there was.

Not maid of honor.

Kate hadn't wanted to hurt Kelsey or Cora's feelings, the other half of their quad-sized friend group, so they were all bridesmaids, each with a different job.

But that was Kate.

Kind. Sweet. Inclusive. In a word, the absolute best.

That was two, or *three*, Heidi, supposed, but the point still stood. Kate was awesome and her best friend in the whole world.

And now she was *married*.

God, they were all growing up. Sniff.

She hated it.

Still, her heart was full, and she sniffed again, dashing away a tear as the officiant declared the newlyweds officially married before they strode down the aisle hand-in-hand.

Heidi followed, striding—hand-in-leash?—with the rooster.

And, well, if that wasn't an apt description of her dating life . . . she didn't know what was. She could find a man who wanted to sleep with her—cough, *cock*—but couldn't find one with staying power.

"Not the point," she muttered under her breath, somehow getting herself and Sir Fuzzy McFeatherston safely down the aisle. The rest of the bridal party paired off and followed her.

They snapped some pictures, but eventually the Fuzz got tired of the paparazzi, and Heidi wrestled him into her arms, taking him to the crate Kate had ready for him.

She was just bending to place him inside—while trying to slip off the harness without letting him escape—when she felt someone come up behind her. Assuming it was Kate, she said, "I'm fine, Katie girl. Go enjoyed your husband. I've got your"— she giggled, a twelve-year-old at heart—"cock well in hand."

Silence instead of her friend's cackling.

*Shit.*

Heat stained her cheeks, and Heidi yanked the leash and harness out before slamming and locking the cage. Then she shored her spine and spun around.

Tall. Dark. A smirk on a gorgeous mouth.

One that grew as his gaze traced her down then up. "Sure you can handle that cock, baby?"

She *had* handled that cock.

Six months ago, Jaime's brother Brad had stopped in the Bay Area for a quick visit, and she'd had a few too many glasses of wine. He'd offered her a ride home . . . and then he'd given her a fucking *ride*.

So yeah, she'd had that cock, and she couldn't lie, it had been *incredible*.

But . . . he'd been gone before she'd woken the next morning.

And she might be tough on the outside, she might be a strong, independent woman who hadn't been expecting a ring and a relationship, but she'd thought she at least warranted a note or a text or a fucking goodbye.

Heidi sniffed. "I've had plenty of cocks in my life," she said, chin lifting, eyes narrowing. "And none are more than I can handle."

She pushed past him.

He snagged her arm.

She yanked it free, stepped back when he went to grab her again. "Don't," she snapped. "Just because I made a mistake once doesn't mean I'm easy prey now."

A cocky—no pun intended *this* time—smile. "Mistake? I happened to think we were—"

"*That* was your mistake," she said, glaring. "*Thinking.*"

Pretty hazel eyes flared. "Baby—"

"Not. Your. Baby."

A sigh. "Heidi."

"Yes, Brad, the groomsman who should be paying attention to his brother's wedding instead of bothering a woman who *isn't interested?*" It wasn't a sweet question, for as sickly saccharine as her tone was.

"I think—"

She rolled her eyes. "Not *that* again."

Heidi didn't mean to. It just . . . it all happened so fast.

Brad grabbed her arm.

She shoved him back at the same time the crate door burst open, and Sir Fuzzy McFeatherston shot out of the pen.

The rooster took off running.

Brad lost his footing, crashed into a waiter, who was carrying a large tray of appetizers.

The food went flying.

*Brad* went flying . . . into the cake table.

*Sir Fuzzy McFeatherston* went flying, feathers scattering in all directions.

The tray came down.

And Heidi didn't think she'd ever forget the sound of it colliding with Brad's head.

Nor how much joy it gave her.

At least until she took a step back, promptly tripped over the fucking rooster . . . and ended up sprawled across Brad's chest.

Fuck, she loved that chest.

# TWO

Heidi

"I AM SO, SO, *SO* SORRY," she said, wiping cake off her temple. "I—"

Kate giggled and swiped a finger through the frosting currently occupying space on her cheek. "I told you, it's fine. The Fuzz is a naughty rooster, and I should have known better than to think he would behave at a wedding of all places."

Heidi grabbed her friend's hands. "He was the cutest ring bearer ever."

Kate's face softened, and she pulled free to grab another towel from the counter of the tiny bathroom they'd sequestered themselves in after the cake debacle, dampening it and working at the frosting embedded in one of Heidi's curls. "He was, wasn't he?"

Heidi snagged the towel and nudged her friend toward the door. "Go, babe. Enjoy your big party." She forced a smile. "I'll do my best to not ruin anything else."

"Heid—"

She reached for the handle, tugged open the wooden panel, nudged her friend out into the hall. The music vibrated through the airwaves, punctuated by laughter and conversation. "Go. Dance yourself into sweaty exhaustion. I'll be out once I'm frosting free."

Kate hesitated.

"*Go.* This is your night. I'm fine."

With a nod and a squeeze of Heidi's arm, Kate disappeared down the hall, her dress swishing and sparkling in her wake.

Her friend was a goddess.

Thankfully, Jaime realized how lucky he was and treated Kate right.

Which meant Heidi didn't have to kill him.

Snorting to herself, she closed the door, going back to work on her frosting-filled curls, and eventually just gave up on her half-up, half-down hairdo and started to take bobby pins out, lining them up neatly on the counter.

The door opened as she had her chin tucked to her chest, staring at the line of pins on the white granite while fighting with a pin stuck right at her nape.

"Go party, Katie," she said, fingers trying and failing to grasp the little folded piece of metal. "I'm fine."

Fingers on her nape, tugging the bobby pin out.

"Thank—" She glanced up and saw that it wasn't Kate in the bathroom with her, guilt drawing her back from her own party to help Heidi out.

It was *him.*

Brad.

Brother of the groom, best lay of her life, and a complete and utter player who was . . . looking at her like he wanted them to play all over again.

Look, she couldn't lie. A part of her wanted that—wanted

the hot, sweaty sex, wanted him to hoist her up onto the counter, lift her dress, and plunge home, over and over again. But the rest of her still had *some* self-respect left. She was smart and reasonably pretty. She couldn't hold her booze, but she *was* a funny drunk on the odd occasion she got that far. Plus, she could cook a mean meatloaf, bake killer chocolate chip cookies, and she always made coffee for herself and whoever stayed over —whether it be friend or fuck—first thing in the morning.

Heidi was more of a catch than not.

And she was tired of being with people who didn't recognize that.

So there would be no hoisting onto counters or dress-lifting. And the man certainly wouldn't be getting any of her special chocolate chip cookies *or* expensive, caffeine-laden coffee.

He reached up to grab another pin, and she smacked his hand away. "You can go."

A slow, sexy smile. "I made the mess. I don't mind cleaning it up."

"I guess I wasn't clear." She kept her back to him, glaring at him in the mirror. "*Go away.*"

Silence.

But he didn't move. She could feel him at her spine filling up the small bathroom, didn't know how she could have ever thought he was Katie. The man *exuded* pure heat and sexually, and . . . the fucker just standing there had her lady parts all perked and at the ready, his mere presence a temptation all its own—

U.G.H.

No.

Her fingers went back to her hair, plucking out pins left and right, pretending he wasn't there . . . even as she felt him in every cell.

"So, I was thinking—"

She snorted. The man just couldn't *stop* thinking.

"—that I should go out and buy a cake for Jaime and Kate."

Unbidden, she felt her heart give a little squeeze before she shored it back up, before she slapped a heavy chain and padlock around it, protecting the bruised organ. "I already Instacarted one." She picked up her purse, digging past the various items that had made up her bride emergency kit—clear nail polish for runs in stockings, safety pins, Band-Aids, wet wipes, energy bars, and more—for her cell. Feeling like she should cheer when she managed to retrieve her phone from that black hole, she tapped a finger on the screen, checked on the cake's process. "See?" She turned, showing him the screen. "It should be here in fifteen minutes."

His eyes changed, emotions mixing in them that she couldn't read, but then he shifted back slightly. "Ah."

Right.

She gave him her back again, set her cell down, and focused back on her hair, searching for any bobby pins that might be hiding in the heavy, dark locks. Not finding any, she resumed her patting, scrubbing, and picking at the frosting that had hardened into her curls during the time she'd spent trying to save her friend's wedding.

Capturing the freaking rooster—who was far more agile and much quicker than she was—and wrestling him into the cage, double-checking that the lock was properly secured the second time around.

Righting the cake table and managing to salvage one tier, so at least Kate and Jaime would be able to cut *something* that resembled a wedding cake for pictures.

Getting ice for the pain-in-the-ass's head who was still standing behind her.

And finally, with frosting and cake bits coating the gorgeous purple dress Kate had picked out for all the bridesmaids, she'd attempted to salvage her outfit.

And hair.

And makeup.

All of which were proving to be . . . unsalvageable.

Fingers in her hair making her shiver, making her hate herself for that shiver. Brad tugged out a pin she'd missed and set it on the counter. "I—" he began.

"Will you just fuck off?" she snapped, slapping her hands down onto that granite and glaring at him in the mirror again. "I get I was an easy fuck a few months ago, but I'm not going to be one again. I get that it was good, but what I *don't* get is how it's always so fucking *easy* for men to walk away from me." She blinked, wishing she could take that last part back. Unfortunately, since she didn't possess time-traveling abilities, she pressed on. "A note," she said. "That's all it would have taken. Just a simple goodbye, rather than skulking off before the sun rose like I'm some little dirty, shameful secret."

Hazel eyes holding hers in the reflection.

He had a colored streak of frosting on his left cheek, though his white shirt was almost pristine. Probably because his suit jacket had taken the brunt of the purple and cream-colored cake.

Stupid men. Could just strip off their jackets and look perfectly normal.

"You're right," he said after a long, tense moment. "I'm sorry. I should have left a note or said goodbye."

An apology.

Just like that.

Then he smiled—slow and hot and thigh-quiveringly sexy. "But in fairness to me, I've had some . . . unpleasant morning interactions." A shrug. "Sometimes it's better for everyone if I just leave."

And just like that, back to the cocky asshole.

She stifled a sigh. "Goodbye, Brad."

Then she focused all her attention on the towel and the sink and not the man behind her, nor on her nipples that were perky in memory of the horizontal yummy time, nor on her vagina that was feeling empty and neglected because she was ignoring its urges.

"I—"

"*Goodbye.*"

After several moments, he released a breath and she watched him out of the corner of her eye as he left the bathroom, the door *clicking* closed softly behind him.

"Thank God," she whispered, going back to work with the towel and warm water, and by the time her cell buzzed with the alert that the delivery driver was approaching with the cake, she had at least managed to de-frosting her hair. Her dress was hopeless. She'd scraped everything off, but the buttercream had left greasy stains all over the bodice and skirt.

Dry-cleaning might salvage it, but she didn't have a change of clothes at her disposal.

So, she was embracing the stains.

Stashing the dirty towels in the basket next to the sink, she turned to the door, opened it, and—

Froze.

A white dress shirt was hanging on the outside of the knob, a note peeking out of the breast pocket.

*Can't change the past, but maybe this note will help.*

-B

Her heart did that squeezing thing, but she shoved it down again, ignoring the stutter, pretending she hadn't even had it in the first place. This didn't mean she was going to forgive the man, and she certainly wasn't going to give him a second chance.

No fucking way.

But she *was* going to use the shirt to cover the worst of the stains. She slipped it from the hanger, buttoned it up, not fully appreciating how much bigger Brad was than her until the starched cotton was surrounding her, engulfing her in his spicy, male scent, the fabric soft against her skin and hanging to her knees, the sleeves draping past her fingertips. It was intoxicating to be wrapped up in him, in the shirt that was still warm from his body.

"It's probably not even his," she muttered, rolling up the sleeves.

But something inside her knew it was, and that inclination was confirmed when she walked out into the area where the reception was being held and saw him dancing with Cora, clad in just a skin-tight white T-shirt.

Ignoring the dance floor, she slipped out to the front of the building, meeting the delivery woman, and then thinking perhaps she went overboard with the cake ordering. Still, she managed to heft the three huge sheet cakes—chocolate, lemon, and vanilla, her attempt to recreate the flavors of the delicious- ness she'd toppled—thanked the woman who was her savior, and headed back to the wedding.

Arms slipped around her, Brad deftly—*somehow*—scooping the cakes out of her hold before she could react or protest or dodge away.

The cakes were worth their weight in gold at this point.

But before she could snatch them back or demand . . . he do *something,* there were hot words in her ear.

"You look good in my shirt."

Words that left her gaping.

And shivering with remembered pleasure, dammit.

Brad was a No Fuck Zone. She'd learned her lesson. Or at least she *should* have learned her lesson.

But nonetheless, she shivered again when those hot hazel eyes met hers and he said, voice husky and feeling like roughened velvet brushing over her skin, "For the record, I wish I'd stayed."

# THREE

Brad

HE SHOULD HAVE STAYED.

He'd known he would regret slipping from beneath those soft cotton sheets, out from Heidi's embrace, moving away from her even softer skin.

But he'd also needed to go.

Not even because he'd had a flight to catch—which he *had* because he always had a flight to catch. He traveled every spare day, spent every extra dollar he had to fly around the world, visiting every sight that had ever caught his fancy. And he'd had a great freaking time doing so, never wanted to stop.

But Heidi was the first woman he'd ever spent any time with that made him want to stay.

To stay *forever*.

So, he'd gone.

Had returned to the postage-stamp apartment he kept for the infrequent times he was in town, having decided that if he were going to be paying for a home he was hardly in, it might as well be filled with California sunshine rather than Midwest humidity and snow. Then he'd packed his usual bag, grabbed his passport, and had flown to Croatia. But as he'd walked through gorgeous coastal cities and explored mountain lakes and appreciated the beautiful agriculture, he hadn't been able to stop thinking of the gorgeous brunette with hazel eyes that were more green than brown.

He'd thought of her laugh while eating alone.

He'd thought of her shining brown hair fanning out on the pillowcase when he'd gone to sleep at night.

He'd *dreamed* of her sexy, curvy body night after night, had woken hard and aching every morning for weeks.

Until he'd forced himself to compartmentalize the woman away, not only for his own sanity, but for hers. Because he wasn't the type of man who stayed, not for a little while, not forever, no matter how beautiful or smart or wonderful the woman was.

And Heidi was definitely all of those.

But still, as time had gone on, he'd almost convinced himself that he'd imagined the draw he felt toward her. After all these months, after making sure to avoid any interaction that might bring them together during the lead up to the wedding, he'd begun to think that perhaps she wasn't . . . so freaking perfect in every way that mattered to him.

But he hadn't been able to avoid her forever.

He'd walked into the wedding rehearsal the night before and felt every cell in his body stand up in attention.

She was there.

He wanted her.

Thankfully, the men and women had separated early in the evening, and he'd been able to keep his distance. But today, seeing her in that fucking incredible purple dress and the way it hugged her curves, watching her eyes go damp as her friend spoke her vows, laughing at the way she'd embraced walking that stupid fucking rooster up the aisle with its vest and sparkling leash.

Hell, she'd embraced *all* of it. The tears, the rooster, even the aftermath of the cake fiasco.

And he'd found he liked her even more.

Fucking hell.

"Give them back," she growled.

"They're heavy," he countered. "Let me carry them for you."

One dark brow lifted. "And you're saying that me, with my weak, feminine arms, can't manage to carry them?"

"Yup." He preemptively bit back a grin, already anticipating her reaction.

Which didn't disappoint.

She scowled, plump lips pressing flat, and he had the distinct notion that she wanted to stomp her foot.

Either that, or she wanted to kick him in the balls.

Maybe both.

"Where do you want them?" he asked, instead of giving voice to either of those thoughts—or to give her any ideas.

Her scowl deepened, but she just pointed to the former cake table, the one they'd spent some quality time on top of, not long before. The tablecloth had been replaced. The one tier they'd been able to salvage sitting on a plate atop it, along with half of a groom figurine and the bride's legs.

Heidi growled, plucking the horrific scene from the cake and wrapping the sad pieces in a napkin, which she stashed in the bodice of her dress. He didn't even bother looking away, not when he had the great privilege to witness the action of her spreading his shirt wide and sticking her hand between the luscious set of breasts he'd once been up close and familiar with. Then she patted the table before buttoning the shirt back up. "Set them here."

He placed the boxes down.

"My bouquet is on the head table," she said, opening one lid. "Can you grab mine, Cora's, and Kelsey's?"

"Got it." He turned away.

She snagged his arm, tugged him to face her. "Do *not* touch Kate's bouquet," she ordered, eyes flashing. "She's saving it, and I will not ruin another thing of hers."

Brad reached down and lifted her hand, bringing it to his lips. "I won't. I promise."

"Good." She snatched her hand free. "Don't."

Then she spun away, giving him her back again, probably not realizing how tempting the line of her nape was with curls teasing the creamy length of skin, nor how her curves were highlighted by the way they pressed against the fabric of his shirt.

He wasn't going to tell her.

For one, he appreciated the view. For another, he appreciated his balls right where they currently resided.

Dodging the dancers on the rented floor, he made his way to the head table and scooped up the proper bouquets—and not the big one with ribbons and a floofy—was that a technical term? Probably not, but it was the only way he could think to describe the flouncing greenery, ribbons, and flowers. Regardless, it only took him a few minutes to return to the cake table, bunches in hand.

What he returned to was . . . amazing.

Heidi had managed to stack the rectangular cakes on top of one another, angling them artistically. The boxes were on the floor next to her feet, and she'd commandeered another flower arrangement from somewhere and was currently placing the buds around the cakes.

"Um," he said, setting the bouquets on the table. "Are you a magician or something?"

She stuck a rose into a gap, not looking at him as she

continued placing flowers, adding in ones from the bunches he'd brought over. "Nope."

Okay then. Apparently, this woman could hold a grudge and a half.

Not that he could really blame her.

Most women didn't appreciate being used—and even if that wasn't what he'd intended, that was what she'd thought.

So, he knew he deserved the frosty reception.

He just . . . didn't like it.

Stifling a sigh, he bent and picked up the boxes, folding them and stowing them beneath the table. "Maybe a more appropriate question would be, how did you learn to do that?"

"It's a hobby." A beat as she dismantled her bouquet, tucking in tulips and roses at regular intervals.

"What other hobbies do you have?"

Hazel eyes on his, condescension in their depths. "Really?" she asked. "We're really going to have this conversation?"

"Are you always so prickly?"

A sigh was his only response.

He bit back a smile. "Your hair looks nice."

She sniffed.

"Heidi."

She froze, head tilting up to the sky, hair floating behind her like some curly brown cloud, her throat exposed and tempting. His mouth watered, actually watered, remembering how he'd dragged his lips over that gentle slope, how he'd traced his tongue along the silken skin.

"I truly am sorry."

Her head flopped to the side, tilting enough so she could meet his gaze. "And I truly meant what I said." She straightened, eyes serious. "I'm not interested. I want someone who wants me enough to stick around." A shrug. "The truth is that I know you well enough by now to know you're not that kind of man."

That stung.

But he couldn't deny it, couldn't pretend she was wrong.

He *didn't* have staying power.

"I know."

Her expression changed, and he hated that *he* didn't know *her* well enough to discern the undercurrent in it. At any rate, she focused her attention back on the cakes, and he watched in silence as she turned the supermarket confections into something that belonged in a fancy bakery.

"I wish I'd ordered icing, too," she murmured, perching a final gathering of blooms on the salvaged tier, which she hadn't stacked on the others, but had somehow made its separation seem intentional with the way she'd arranged the flowers.

"It looks beautiful."

She froze, almost as though she'd forgotten he was there.

He was so attuned to her that he didn't think it would be possible to *not* be aware of her. Ever since he'd walked into the church the night before—*no*. Since the moment he'd joined in on that dinner all those months ago, tagging along with Jaime and Kate to meet up with Heidi, Cora, and Kelsey, he hadn't been able to get this smart, gorgeous woman out of his brain.

Brad couldn't even say it was because she came in a beautiful package—though he certainly appreciated her curves, her pretty face with those expressive eyes and kissable lips. But his fascination had begun at that dinner and had only grown through the night. When Kelsey had been picked up by her fiancé, Tanner, and Cora had left with Kate and Jaime because they all lived close, he'd offered her a ride ostensibly because his apartment was close to her place, but in truth, because he'd wanted to spend more time with her.

Yes, he was attracted to her.

But that attraction wasn't just sexual. She was witty and more than once, she'd made some offhand comment that had him bursting into laughter. Beyond that, he could tell she was a good person who cared about the people at that table—including him.

Because he was related to Jaime. Because Jaime was smitten, and because he made Kate happy.

So, he'd had an in, and he'd been attracted to her.

And . . . they'd ended up in bed. And the sex had been incredible. And he'd—

"Ruined," she murmured.

Brad blinked for a moment, wondering if she'd picked the thought from his mind or perhaps if he'd spoken aloud. But she wasn't looking at him. She was staring down at the cake, a sour expression on her face.

Then she sighed and rolled her shoulders, exposing her neck as she stretched her head from side to side again. Tempting him. Again.

"Oh well," she said, straightening on another sigh. "I've done what I can." She fussed with one more flower then stepped back. "I should find Fuzzy McFeatherston and make sure he doesn't get within a hundred feet of this."

"I took him home."

Her lips parted, and it took everything in him to not taste her. "What?"

"I figured it was safer to get him back to his coop at Kate and Jaime's." Which had been convenient, considering the venue they'd chosen to hold the reception at was only twenty minutes from their house.

"You left for forty minutes?"

He glanced at his watch. "Fifty-six," he said, "But who's counting? Especially when you're wiping frosting out of your curls."

Her lips tipped up into a smile that he felt all the way to his cock. Then she sobered, "But it's your brother's wedding."

"I snuck out while they were taking their individual pictures, snuck back in when you and Kate were doing your thing." He shrugged. "Also, I couldn't exactly just shove him in the back of my car, could I? And clearly, the cage couldn't be trusted to hold him securely."

That much was true.

"Oh." A beat. "Well, I should—"

The music changed, the heavy beat of a fast-paced dance anthem melting into a slow melody, into an unhurried ballad that coaxed couples to the floor, that made the hot, sweaty atmosphere shift into something intimate and hushed.

"Dance with me," he said.

She shook her head, those curls bouncing. "I shouldn't—"

"We're a bridesmaid and groomsman," he coaxed, nodding toward Kelsey and Cora, both of whom were twirling with other members of the bridal party, and Jaime and Kate, who were in the center of the mix, looking blissfully happy. "We should be out there."

White teeth nibbling into a pink-painted bottom lip.

He took a risk . . . and took her hand.

# FOUR

Heidi

WARM FINGERS LACED WITH HERS, a slightly calloused thumb stroking across her palm.

Back and forth. Back and forth. Back and—

Then she was pressed to Brad's chest, the heat of his body surrounding her, her breasts tingling as they brushed against the hard muscles of his torso. The sneaky man had maneuvered her into the dance on the back patio of the restaurant Kate and Jaime had rented out without her recognizing it, like a mesmerizing hand-ninja who'd stroked her palm and all of a sudden, she was in his arms, his body coaxing hers into sensually unhurried motion. A shiver skating down her spine when he slid his hand down, the heat of him seeping through the layers of his shirt and her dress, imprinting onto her skin.

"I—"

"I love this song," he said softly.

She blinked, surprised that he'd admit to liking the poppy ballad. "Really?"

"What can I say? I'm a Gaga fan." He smiled, slow and sexy. "The woman's got pipes."

Lips parting, she scrambled to say something. Hell, to say *anything*.

But nothing came.

Which seemed to suit him just fine. He just tucked her closer and swayed them to the music.

"Why are you doing this?" she whispered.

Silence as they moved to the music. Silence for long enough that she thought he wouldn't answer. But then as the chorus ramped up, he murmured, "I'd like us to be friends."

Now it was her turn for silence.

Then . . . she burst out laughing.

Probably not the wisest thing to do in the middle of the dance floor, the music soft enough that her outburst garnered attention. But she couldn't help it. The man was going to be an A-list comic if he thought that was even in the realm of possibility.

She glanced up, lifting a palm from his chest—how had that gotten there?—and using her fingers to wipe the tears forming at the corners of her eyes.

His pretty hazel irises were focused on her, the golden and green deepened to a rich brown with the twinkling lights and navy sky above them. "That's a no, then?"

"That's a no."

He nodded, his eyes on hers as the song wound down, as a faster one took its place, the DJ breaking into it with the announcement that the cake cutting would begin in just a couple of minutes.

"I should—" she began.

Another nod, his arms slipping from around her, one hand grasping her elbow as he led them off the floor. Once on the side, he kissed her cheek, making her breath hitch and her heart skip a beat as his heat came close again, as his scent—spicy and earthy and tempting—filled her nose.

"I should have said goodbye," he whispered.

And then he was gone, walking away, his broad shoulders stretching the white cotton to alluring degrees, his stride purposeful as he disappeared into the restaurant that Kate and Jaime had rented out.

The urge to follow him was strong.

*Really* strong.

But the moment she actually gave in to the temptation to follow him, the moment she took a single step in his direction, Kate came up and grabbed her arm. Saving her from doing something incredibly idiotic. "Did you do that?"

Run off the sexy, gorgeous man who clearly wanted to give her another glorious night of sexy time?

Yes, she had done that.

But out of self-preservation.

Because . . . self-worth and value and . . . some other things that were important for some reason. She blinked, shook her head. No, not for *some* reason. They were important for her to keep hold of her self-respect, not to mention her feminist card.

But it turned out that Kate wasn't staring after the gorgeous Brad.

She was looking at the cake table, the mishmash of flowers and supermarket cakes she'd thrown together.

Heidi winced. "Yeah. I know it's not—"

Kate hugged her tight. "Why the hell did I spend that much money on an expensive cake when you could create *that?*"

"It's not—"

Kate released her. Then promptly gripped Heidi's chin between thumb and forefinger. "You are an amazing friend, and I love you."

Shit.

Now Heidi's eyes stung.

And then they were hugging each other, and yeah, so maybe it was mostly because Kate was deliriously happy—and perhaps had consumed one too many of the signature cocktails—but Heidi was still emotional. "I love you, too, Katie girl," she whispered then nudged her friend back. "Now, go find that sexy husband of yours and let's cut some cake!"

"Holy shit," Kate breathed. "Husband? *Husband*. I'm *married!*"

Heidi grinned. "You are, honey."

Kate did a little dance. "And now I get to eat cake."

"The literal embodiment of having your cake and eating it, too."

"Precisely." A grin. A kiss to her cheek. And one more squeeze that hurt Heidi's heart—in the best way. "I'm going to go find my husband."

Heidi nodded her chin behind Kate's shoulder. "I don't think you have to do much searching."

Not that the happy couple heard her.

They were smiling and staring into each other's eyes in a way that should have been sickening, but she couldn't fault her friend for that type of love, even if Jaime had regrown his man bun solely because Kate demanded it.

The man had nice hair, but—Heidi shuddered—she just couldn't get behind man buns.

And she digressed down the rabbit hole of unnecessary thoughts.

Luckily for her, the DJ called the guests to attention at that moment, directing everyone to the cake table for the cutting ceremony. Heidi caught a glimpse of Brad—because, of course, he wouldn't miss an important part of the wedding. People could say what they wanted about the wayward traveler, but when he was in town, he was a good brother.

He had good qualities, she supposed.

His family, Jaime included, were great.

But she supposed he was also a decent person—the sneaking-out-of-bed-before morning-problem aside. And really, as much as she wanted to be mad at him about that, she *had* invited him into her townhouse, she *had* wanted him, she *had* slept with him. Because she'd made that choice. Had she anticipated something different for the morning after? Fuck yes, she had. Did it hit a little too close to home because she was feeling vulnerable and the sneaking out he'd pulled hadn't been the first time that had happened to her?

Also, yes.

Did she still really want to hold it against him? Yup.

Did she understand that was unreasonable? Sigh. Also, yup.

But was she going to sleep with him again? That was a no.

A big, fat no.

Her gaze drifted from Kate and Jaime, posed with their hands intertwined on the knife, the blade poised above the frosting, to Brad, sexy in a freaking T-shirt and slacks, a slight scruff on his sharp jawline that she'd spent serious time kissing. He was too fucking pretty, and she hated herself for wanting him.

And maybe she hated herself even more for wanting to skirt the crowd, to take his hand, and lead him into that tiny bathroom for some counter-hoisting and skirt-lifting.

But while Heidi might be a lot of things—book smart, successful, a decent person—she wasn't a liar.

Including to herself.

So, when Brad's eyes shifted from the cake cutting to hers and her breath caught, heat curling in her abdomen, need flaring anew, she embraced that she would always feel that want, that the attraction would always be there.

Because she could also be one more thing.

Incredibly stubborn.

There was no freaking way she would ever open her heart—or body—to Brad again.

# FIVE

## Brad

HE HEARD the soft curse long after he'd thought everyone had left the wedding.

Frowning, he pushed up from the bench where he'd just met with the restaurant manager to make sure the final bills had been taken care of—they had, because Kate and Jaime had planned this wedding down to a tee—and stared out into the dark parking lot, trying to discern where the noise had originated.

"Shit," came another mutter, though this time, it was accompanied by the *click-clicking* of high heels.

He'd been enjoying a moment of quiet after the events of the evening, a few minutes to regroup and reset before he headed home, but the noise had him turning in time to see Heidi exiting the back of the building, presents stacked so high in her arms that he was surprised she could even see enough to navigate the dark walk.

"Here," he said, hurrying over to her.

"Brad?"

"Yup," he answered, snagging the teetering stack of boxes and opening up her vision. "What are you doing?" He'd seen her drive off earlier.

A shrug. "I couldn't fit all of Jaime and Kate's presents in my car. Had to drop them at their house then come back for another trip," she said, shifting the packages and prompting him to take several more gift bags from her arms. That she didn't fight him came as a surprise "Thanks." A smile. "My arms are killing me."

She led the way to her car, opening the trunk once they'd arrived, and after they'd gone back to the gift table for one more load of presents, they began the real-world game of Tetris, trying to see if the remaining packages would fit amongst the ones she'd already loaded.

"Kate and Jaime made out," he said, shoving a gift bag into the one remaining hole.

Heidi was cramming boxes into the front seat. "No kidding," she muttered. "It looks like a Bed, Bath, and Beyond exploded in here."

He laughed.

Then attempted to close the trunk.

His attempt was unsuccessful.

"This isn't working," he said. "Let's load up my car. I'll follow you over."

Heidi's lips parted, and he thought she'd protest, thought she'd bury herself in the driver's seat with presents before she agreed to more of his help, but she surprised him once again, nodding then wedging the passenger's door closed and coming to the rear of her car. "You're right," she said, pulling several packages out.

He snagged a few more, and then they managed to close the hatch.

This time, he led the way to his small hybrid—because there was no point in him keeping a big, fancy car when he was hardly in town—and he and Heidi squeezed the remainder of the bags and wrapped boxes into his car.

"I am *so* glad I don't have to write thank you notes for these," she said dryly.

He laughed. "Me, too."

Then he walked her to her car, said again, "I'll follow you over."

Her eyes came to his, held, and for a moment, he thought he saw some heat in those depths. But it was dark, the moonlight overhead hardly doing anything to illuminate the lot. Shadows and blurred lines. Fantasy in thinking this woman would be anything more than polite to him.

"Okay," she murmured, opening the driver's door and sitting down.

A moment later, the engine was on and he was heading back to his sedan, starting up his own car's engine, and carefully pulling out of his spot then following Heidi through the quiet roads and up the winding street that led to the small ranch-style house that Jaime and Kate had bought on the outskirts of town.

Mostly because Kate wanted *all* the animals.

Including the freaking rooster, who'd caused no shortage of pandemonium.

Last he'd heard, they had adopted a trio of goats that had been destined for slaughter, Fuzzy McFeatherston, the evil rooster, and his half-dozen harem of hens, two dogs, three cats, and a turtle.

At least his brother was a vet, so they didn't have to worry about bills from that front.

But bills coming from the *human* baby front?

If Brad were a betting man, he'd say those would be coming soon.

Heidi turned into the driveway, and he followed her, making

sure to leave enough room between the cars so the doors could open all the way. They'd need all avenues of maneuverability in order to get these presents out of the cars and into the house.

A moment later, Heidi was out of her sedan and ladening herself with packages.

He popped his door.

"Will you use the keypad and open the door?" she asked, gift bags lined up on her arms like oversized bracelets. "The code is—"

"I know it," he said, grabbing a few boxes before high-tailing it up the walk.

He punched in the code, pushed inside, and dropped his burden with the rest of the presents in the living room then went back outside. Along the way, he made sure the latch was open, but not the door—because he didn't want to be responsible for kitty escapes.

Heidi was coming up the steps, so he doubled-back, opened the door for her, did his whole latch but not wide-open procedure, then returned to his car.

They repeated the process, unloading the presents and stacking them inside the house, until that front room appeared to have become the landing ground for every shade of sparkling silver wrapping paper and the entire stockpile from the tissue paper industry.

When they were done, Heidi set the alarm and they closed the front door behind them.

"The pet-sitter will be here in the morning."

"Hopefully the cats don't get into the bags."

She winced. "I didn't think of that."

"How much trouble can they get into?" he asked.

Another wince. "Have you met the Terrible Two?"

"No, why?"

Her lips twitched. "They make the Fuzz look like the most well-behaved rooster you've ever seen."

His brows lifted.

"I'm not joking."

"Shit."

Her shoulders slumped as she turned back to the door. "Maybe I'll lock the cats in Jaime and Kate's room, and tomorrow I can come back to move the presents into the spare bedroom and lock the door."

"I can help you move them now," he offered.

"I'm tired," she said, chin dropping to her chest. "And my feet hurt."

He nudged her toward her car. "Go home," he ordered.

"I—"

"You took care of Cake-Gate," he said. "I can deal with Present-Gate. Plus, there's no telling if we'll be able to find or catch the cats."

Her nose wrinkled. "That's true. But I should really—"

"Go home and rest?" he said, guiding her to her car. "Yes, *that*."

"But—" He opened the driver's door, and still she hesitated.

Another nudge had her sitting in the seat, and he closed the metal panel as soon as her feet were clear, trapping her inside.

"Drive home. Get sleep," he said loud enough so she could hear him.

She made a face but didn't protest further, just turned her car on and backed out of the driveway. Brad watched the taillights disappear down the street then went back into the house and got his workout moving those packages from the living room into the guest bedroom, making sure he closed the door securely to prevent any kitty escapades.

Then he drove home.

And when he finally made it into bed, after a long, hot

shower that washed the remnants of cake and frosting from his body, he dreamed of silken brown hair fanning out on the pillow beside him.

———

THE MONDAY FOLLOWING THE WEDDING, he pulled into the underground parking garage then made his way up to his apartment.

His lonely, *empty* apartment.

Funny how he'd never much minded the tiny unit with its drab lighting and noisy upstairs neighbors. Usually, it was just a stopover to the next adventure.

Except . . . he didn't have any more adventures planned.

And the itchy feeling, the one that usually crept in after a few weeks home, coaxing him off into the sunset, was noticeably absent.

Instead, he was drawn in a different direction.

Drawn toward one person in particular.

"Which just confirms what you already know," he muttered, fighting with the old lock for a moment before he managed to let himself into his apartment. "Heidi is the best thing you've ever come across."

Small and dark were the apartment's best qualities—aside from kickass internet, that was. The rest of it, he'd done his best with. A cheap couch that was covered in a tapestry he'd picked up in Peru. Several prints from a local artist in Iceland on the far wall—mostly so he could pretend there was another window there. His bed was behind a screen he'd purchased in Japan. His shelves were made by an artist in Indonesia, who'd collected driftwood washed up onshore.

His life in objects, and yet none of them could fill the hole inside him.

None of them told him who he was.

But then again, why did he need to be told?

Now *there* was the itchy feeling, rearing its ugly head, making him think too much, feel too much.

Jaime was the caring one. Tammy was the smart one. Penny was the go-getter. And he was . . .

What?

Driven by fancy? Lacking attention and focus?

He knew neither of the last two were true, and if there was any fancy involved, it was from simply wanting to make the most of every moment, because he undertook a great deal of planning with his trips, ensuring he didn't waste his money or his opportunity to visit.

"Fucking hell," he muttered, going to the one window in the space. It was half-blocked by the refrigerator, but it provided fresh air and sunlight, and most importantly, a way out.

A fire escape that led up to the roof.

Yanking open the panel, he clambered ungracefully out the frame, grasping onto the metal ladder and climbing.

It was late, and he didn't want to be that creeper outside of someone's apartment, freaking them out, so he moved quickly and quietly up the ladder, past the other windows, until he'd ascended the three floors above him and reached the roof. Not too long ago he'd stashed a blanket on the rooftop space that was definitely not approved by management, adding it to the chair and the lamp other people had brought. Tonight, however, he wanted to feel the chill on his skin, so he hauled himself over the ledge, straightened, and looked up at the sky.

God, he'd seen it in so many iterations, the stars in different alignments depending on what side of the globe or which hemisphere he was in, but somehow it still brought him comfort.

There were bigger things out there than him and his small life—no matter how big he tried to make it.

His cell rang.

He answered without bothering to glance at the screen. Only his family and a few old friends had this number.

"Brad," Jaime said, sounding blissfully happy. "I'm surprised that you're not somewhere without an internet connection."

Considering he'd spent a fair amount of the last decade in exactly that scenario, he didn't comment except to say, "I'm here." Of course, it wasn't until after he'd spoken the two words that he realized his tone was all wrong.

Silence.

"What's wrong?"

Shit.

"Nothing," he said, forcing his tone to be his normal cheerful. "I went to Coit Tower today, and it was . . . well, it was a big tower in the middle of the city, and yesterday I went to this beach—"

"Brad."

Double shit.

Now he'd triggered both Jaime's oldest brother side *and* his intuitive he-cares-for-animals-who-can't-talk vet caring side.

Which basically meant, Brad was in for it now.

"How's the honeymoon?" he asked instead, going for diversion. He didn't want to hash through what was in his head. Not when he felt like it might be the key to a lot of the shit that had twisted him up for so long.

"The honeymoon's great," Jaime said. "Except for a certain younger brother, who thinks that he can get that shit of an attempt at distraction past me. "What's going on?"

"Seriously. I'm fine."

"And *that's* horseshit. What's up? Your flight to your future destination get canceled?"

"I'm staying in California."

"For a few more weeks until we get back?" His brother sounded thrilled. "That's great, we can catch up some more before you fly off again."

"No."

"Oh." Disappointed now. "But at least with you living so close, we can hang out during the times you're back."

"No, Jaim." Brad sighed. "I mean, I'm staying in California permanently. I'm thinking that most of my traveling days are at an end."

A beat then, "Who are you, and what have you done to my brother?"

He sighed. Of course, Jaime wouldn't understand. Brad barely knew what was going through his head himself. All he knew was that he wanted Heidi, he wanted something more permanent and fixed, he wanted a place to live that wasn't a tiny, dark, questionably clean apartment, where he could build something that wasn't fueled by excitement for the next grand thing out there.

He wanted to be happy with who and where and what he was now.

Because . . . he had a feeling he'd spent all these years running.

"Brad?" Jaime asked. "Did I lose you?"

He clenched his jaw, released it. "No, I'm here."

Jaime's voice gentled. "I was just kidding, you know."

Forcing a laugh, he said, "I know. It's fine. How's the resort?"

"The reason I won't ever seriously complain about all your traveling," Jaime told him. "Being sequestered here with Kate is definitely no hardship."

"Is it as good as I remember?"

"Better."

Brad hadn't stayed on site—it was a bit too expensive and

catering for his tastes, especially for a single man traveling by himself. But it *was* perfect for a honeymooning couple who'd deserved plenty of pampering, pool-side service, and good restaurants for whenever they decided to emerge from their room.

"But just because I'm getting copious amounts of exercise with my beautiful wife—and I don't mean in the gym—"

"I never thought you did," he muttered.

"Just because I'm having copious amounts of glorious sex with my lovely wife," he corrected, "doesn't mean my brain has rotted. I know something is up with you. So, out with it already. Otherwise we'll both be here all night."

"I can just hang up."

"I'll call back." A pause. "Or I'll sic Mom on you."

Sighing and rubbing the throb that had mysteriously appeared in his temple, he tried something else. "Look, I'm just a little tired tonight. I stayed up late working on a project and . . ."

"And what?" Jaime pressed.

"Did you ever wish you were different?"

*That* hadn't been the thought he'd been forming in his mind, the words he was trying to pull together were going to be more along the lines of something to put his brother at ease, a way to move on with this conversation. But, as silence greeted him over the airwaves, Brad realized it was the most important question.

The thing that was at the crux of everything.

Why the souvenirs from his travel meant so much, but also made him feel sad by reminding him that he'd missed out on a lot.

He'd had grand adventures, but he'd used them to build his identity, until that identity was more *him* than he was.

He was *that* guy—the one too busy looking to the future to

appreciate the now. Hell, he'd been too enamored of that future to be anything but *terrified* of the now.

But the thought that was nagging at him was *why*.

Why was he terrified to be present, to be fully in this moment?

Was it because it might not live up to expectations? Or . . . was it something else?

And why *didn't* he know? Shouldn't he understand what was going on in his own brain?

Seriously. Why the fuck didn't he understand what was going on in his brain?

"Different how?" Jaime asked quietly.

Brad blinked away the thoughts, the questions that, at that time, were frustratingly unnerving and unanswerable.

"I'm not sure," he admitted.

"That's not an answer."

A bolt of anger shot through him, and a retort was actually on the tip of his tongue before he bit it back. This wasn't his brother's fault. It was his own irritation that he couldn't understand the tangle in his mind and heart, when he wanted to be clearheaded in both.

"I *want* to answer you," he said, voice tempered. "But I don't fucking know *how*."

Jaime released a long, slow breath, sending static through the speakers of Brad's cell. "Mom always told me you're the one she worries the most about."

Somehow disappointed by that reply, somehow wanting his big brother to have the proverbial answer to the flurry of thoughts and concerns and questions in his mind, even though it wasn't like *he* was doling out exceptional wisdom in this conversation with all his *I don't knows* and *I don't know hows*, he sank down into the chair on that roof, the coolness that lingered on the plastic seeping in through his jeans, chilling the backs of his thighs, and forced out a cordial response. "Well, that makes sense," he said. "I have traveled to some pretty sketchy places in my time."

A beat of quiet.

Then, "Ask me when she told me that."

Something in his brother's tone had Brad sitting up a little straighter, tearing his eyes from the stars overhead and shifting them to the roof of the opposite building, even though he wasn't really processing the rectangular lines. Instead, he stared at it, almost unseeing, a feeling of foreboding pressing heavily on him, anticipating that he was about to learn something monumental.

"When?" he asked, the question barely audible, even to his own years.

A long pause. "When she was sick."

Brad inhaled sharply.

Their mom had been diagnosed with cancer when Brad was eight. He remembered it being a terrifying time, with her being in and out of the hospital for surgeries and treatments. She was healthy now, had been in remission for a long, long time, but he didn't think he would ever forget the way she'd looked while in that hospital bed or the sound of her retching after she'd received the chemo.

He'd been worried he might hurt her, had been so afraid to touch her, to hug her.

To get close to her.

Jaime began talking again, intruding on those memories, but Brad was happy to let them go, relieved to be able to shove them down into the locked box in his mind. "I had gone to visit her in the hospital one day. It was when she was really sick, and well, you guys were younger, and I don't think you recognized how touch-and-go it was, so I needed that extra time with her, I guess."

"I knew," Brad whispered.

That feeling sitting heavy in his gut, knowing that he was going to lose the single most important thing in his life. His dad had been around, of course, had been great then, just as he was now, but it wasn't the same as it had been with his mom. There was just something special about moms, he supposed.

And though his parents had tried to shield them from the worst of it, he knew from firsthand experience that the type of battle his mom had fought permeated everything.

*Colored* everything.

"What?" Jaime asked.

Swallowing hard against that recognition, he said, "I knew that she almost died. Not as an adult, but back then as a kid. I *knew*."

His brother was quiet for several moments. "I get that. It was probably hard to try to hide much from any of us, but I guess . . . I'd always assumed that you and Tammy were too young to understand, to truly get how precarious it was." He sighed. "We're lucky she's here."

"Yes, we are."

"I wasn't trying to bring you back there. It's just"—Jaime hesitated—"I swear, I've never forgotten what she told me that day. I just didn't know how it fit in, especially with—" He broke off. "I'd gone after school to see her before soccer practice, and she was white as a fucking ghost, lying there with her eyes closed." His breathing was unsteady for a few heartbeats, and Brad had the sense that his brother was trying to hold on to his typically even-keeled personality in the face of what had to be a really dark memory. "Well, I thought she was dead, and I think I would have run screaming from the room if not for her opening her eyes."

Brad stilled, a chill going through him.

Jaime cleared his throat roughly. "I don't think I'll ever be able to erase that, the way she looked, the horror I felt, and shit, it's been what? Like almost twenty years since she went into remission?"

"About that," he agreed.

"So, she opened her eyes and waved me over, and I sat down next to her, heart pounding, trying to pretend I was totally fine when I was a thirteen-year-old kid pissing his pants and wanting to crawl onto the bed with her, wanting her to just hold me and tell me everything would be okay."

Brad clenched his jaw, eyes stinging.

"Instead, I started pulling out my homework before she even asked—because you *know* she would have asked."

He laughed. "Yes, she definitely would have asked." Their mom had always had her finger on the pulse of their family, somehow recollecting which of the four of them had a project due or a dentist appointment or needed to wear something special for an event at school.

"But she saw right through me. She knew that I was upset, that I was taking it really hard, and she ordered me into bed with her." He released a breath. "I resisted, said I was too big, too old, but she wouldn't let it go. She made it an order until I finally got into bed with her. And then . . . she just wrapped her arms around me and told me everything would be okay."

Brad released a shaky breath.

"We laid like that for a long time, and I remember at some point looking up at the clock and realizing that I had to get to practice, so I packed up my things, got ready to walk my ass over to the field, and then just before I reached the door, she stopped me and said, '*You need to watch out for Brad.*'" Jaime inhaled, released it slowly. "And I remember grabbing onto the door handle and saying something to the effect of '*Why? What do I need to protect myself from?*' Thinking you'd stolen my Legos or were planning some prank, like you were always doing as an eight-year-old little twerp."

That made him smile, enough that he could actually muster a light retort. "You're just saying that because I always got you."

"I'm glaring at you right now." Jaime laughed. "But, yes, *that's* also true. Still, she wasn't talking about the Legos or one of your pranks. Because in response, she told me, '*I worry for your brother because he's the type of person who always seems happy on the surface, and those are the people who are usually hurting the most underneath. That's why you need to watch out for him.*'" Jamie cleared his throat. "You were a kid, a pain in the ass kid, but you weren't ever sad or down or anything other than an annoying kid brother, so I thought she was being ridiculous."

"I probably *was* stealing your Legos or planning something," Brad said lightly, even though his throat was tight, and his heart was pounding in his throat. He actually felt a little dizzy, as though the Earth had just suddenly shifted on its axis.

"That's possibly true," Jaime agreed. "But I've also finally gotten old enough to understand what she was saying . . . and to understand *why* she said it. She put on that good front, *wanted* to kick cancer's ass, but it had to have crossed her mind that she might not be here and that she wanted someone to know . . . well, to know that."

"I—" He struggled with words again.

Was that what he was? What his mom had said? Was he unhappy?

He didn't feel unhappy spending time with Heidi or when he was with his family. He *never* felt unhappy when he was traveling—which was probably why he'd clocked so many hours on planes and in other countries.

"I don't think she was thinking you were sad all the time," Jaime said, "but more that you're really good at putting on a mask. You come across as so easy-going that people don't often recognize that you need more from them." He blew out a breath. "And I think Mom needed me to know in case—"

Pulse pounding in his ears, Brad had to joke.

Because otherwise he might cry.

And God, he really didn't want to cry that night.

"Must be all the gray hairs," he said on a laugh, and even *he* could hear that it didn't sound remotely right. "Mom always said my superpower was giving her new ones hourly."

Jaime chuckled. "It wasn't the gray hairs, though I can't deny that I'm now old enough to find a couple of those now and then." His tone went serious. "But, Brad, it's only because I have Kate now that I understand what Mom was saying then. Because my Kate was one of those people—the ones who seem happy on the surface, but who was hurting underneath."

Heart pounding, Brad couldn't bring himself to form a response.

Which was just as well, because Jaime wasn't done talking.

"So, bro, my question to you is . . . what's beneath the veneer? What's that proverbial grain of sand in the oyster, rubbing you raw? Or maybe it's a big spike that's jabbing at you over and over again, something that's hurting you and just won't go away, no matter how hard you try to ignore it."

"I—" He shook his head even though his brother couldn't see him. It was all he could manage, when all he could think was

. . .

Happy on the surface.

And what was beneath?

Nothing.

Empty.

Unfulfilled.

Fuck, that was gloomy. Fuck, that didn't make him feel better. Fuck, *why* didn't he know what the hell was in his own brain?

"Just think about it," Jaime said. "Okay?"

"Okay," he whispered after a moment. "I will."

They said their goodbyes and hung up, Brad continuing to sit on the chair with the stars overhead, continuing to berate himself for not knowing his own mind. But the problem was that he didn't feel jabbed or raw or even hurt.

He just felt . . . alone.

For the second time in as many minutes, he went completely ramrod stiff, not breathing, not moving as he realized that, no, he wasn't necessarily unhappy or depressed.

He was empty.

Because he'd filled his life with all the wrong things—or perhaps, *most* of the wrong things, because he did have his family. But he didn't have any close friendships, and he'd used traveling as a tool.

To avoid connection.

To avoid getting too close to anyone . . . because if he did get close then he might care about them and they would leave, or they might get sick and die. But if *he* left first, if *he* was too busy or off doing his own thing, then he wouldn't be as hurt.

*That* was why the first night with Heidi had freaked him out so much.

*That* was why he'd run.

Because he'd known she was different, known he couldn't leave her behind.

The only question was whether he had the strength to fill that empty void inside him, whether he had the strength to put that need to keep people at a distance behind him.

Heidi's smile flashed through his mind, the pride on her face when she'd stared up at him with the amazing cake creation to replace the mess he'd made, the tears she'd wiped from her eyes when she'd watched Kate and Jaime kiss at the altar, her joy when she'd caught the bouquet, her arms as she'd walked toward him, the slender limbs laden with presents from the wedding. Hell, even her glares.

None of that had made him feel empty.

None of that had made him feel alone.

"So fuck that," he whispered. "Fuck the void, fuck the distance."

He was done with running.

He was ready to live a life that was so fucking full it was spilling over.

And he wanted to live it with Heidi.

# SIX

Heidi

SIGHING, she shut down her computer and stretched her shoulders, knowing that the calculations weren't quite right but also knowing that she was too tired to sort out where exactly she'd gone wrong.

Gathering up dirty coffee cups and muffin wrappers—her guilty pleasure was the banana chocolate chunk ones from the best bakery in town, *Molly's*—she made sure all the equipment was either shut down or properly collecting data they'd retrieve in the days and weeks to come.

Her assistants had left several hours before, but she was playing catch-up after having had a meeting with the board earlier in the day. Which meant she'd spent more time schmoozing than mathing—and had hated every minute of it.

She understood the need for the schmoozing. She just was never more at home than when she was in her lab. A lab that was hers and hers alone. Well, hers alone if she ignored the fact that the funding came from the company and she had to clear her research with the board members. But for the most part, they left her to her electron microscope, her spectrometer, her calculations.

Aside from the schmoozing.

Thankfully, that only happened quarterly, and the rest of the year, she was left to her own devices, in her own lab. That she was in charge of.

Yup.

She was living the female scientist dream.

When she'd quit her previous job just over a year before, she'd been at a loss. She'd worked at universities and big corporations. But the red tape had been astronomical. And not only that, but she'd felt like every single one of her decisions she'd made, every shred of research and evidence she'd conducted and garnered had been questioned. Ostensibly, she'd been running her own lab for one of the best companies in the world.

And she'd been micromanaged within an inch of her life.

She'd been miserable and ready to change positions—or maybe to go *back* to school and make a bid at becoming a career student.

Then she'd found Volton.

And this company was different. It was still a power in the industry, but it was smaller and run by a CEO who was determined to not let it get bogged down with big company problems.

Which made it a joy to work for.

It was the mystical unicorn of careers to actually love getting up in the morning to come to work, and she was riding that magical, horned horse like a champ, *clomp-clomping* into her lab every weekday morning. And some weekends.

So long as there were coffee and muffins.

Smiling to herself, she placed the dirty mugs in the sink, set the coffee pot to be ready to brew for the morning, and locked up.

Her phone buzzed as she walked to her car, and she pulled

it out of her pocket, smiling wider when she saw that it was Kate texting her a picture of her purple-painted toes dipping into the white sand of a beach.

Typing on the screen as she walked, she sent,

*Why are you wasting time with your precious hubby to text me?*

A beat. Then a buzz.

*To torment you with all the luxury that's surrounding me.*

The words were accompanied by a photo of two massage tables set up on the beach.

Heidi laughed.

*You're evil.*

Then added.

*But you're having a good time?*

Kate's reply came in just a few seconds.

*The best.*

Heidi's heart squeezed.

*I'm glad. Now stop texting me and go enjoy your honeymoon.*

When no reply came, she smiled, stowed the cell in her

pocket, and pushed into the underground garage. Which was the exact moment her phone buzzed again.

"Kate," she muttered, "you just don't learn."

But when she glanced at the screen, the message wasn't from Kate.

It was a call from her mother.

"Good God," she whispered, debating ignoring the call and the ramifications that might bring. Her mom wasn't like Kate's or Jaime's. She wasn't . . . nice, wasn't the type to make cookies or pull up an extra chair at the table for an unexpected guest.

Nope. Her mother was razor sharp.

And fuck did it burn to be on the receiving end of her words.

But she was old enough to understand that a conversation now would save a longer, drawn-out, painful conversation later, so she waved goodbye to the security guard and swiped a finger across the screen as she got into her car.

She didn't drive anywhere though.

Not yet.

Her mother had a way of infuriating her beyond reason, and after one close call too many while trying to ignore exactly how painful her barbs were and the subsequent distraction making Heidi a danger to other drivers, she'd promised herself no vehicular operation under the influence of her mom.

"Hello?" she said.

"Why aren't you at home?"

Her brows drew together. "What do you mean?"

"Your father was at a meeting in the city. We drove by to pick you up for dinner, but you're not home."

"No," she said, not surprised that her mom, Colleen, had shown up without a word, expecting her to drop everything. That was the status quo. "I'm not home. I'm just getting off work."

Saying that was a mistake.

She knew it.

Somehow, she had been dumb enough to say it anyway.

Colleen's sigh was loud. "How are you ever going to get married if you work so much?"

As far as responses went, that was a one on a scale of ten. One meaning the best-case scenario. It wasn't denigrating her career choice, just a simple, almost normal-mom reaction lamenting the fact that she wasn't married.

That was something Kate or Jaime's mom might say.

Or *had* said, since they were married now.

But then the one turned into a . . . six-point-five.

"You know there's a reason female scientists are rare," her mom said. "It's because most of them actually listen to their biological clocks and get out of the field in time before their ovaries dry up."

Ew.

"I love what I do, Mom."

Colleen scoffed.

"And I'm happy being alone."

Another scoff. "No, you're not," she said, and now her voice approached razor blades, approached that ten out of ten on that scale of awful. "You're sad and alone and will always be that way if you don't get your priorities in order."

*Slice.*

"Goodbye, Mom," Heidi whispered and hung up, resting her head on the steering wheel, hating that these conversations left her feeling like this—flayed open, vulnerable, like a little kid who couldn't find her voice.

She wished she could shoot barbs back, stand up for herself better, but every time she thought she had a handle on the conversation, her mom brought mean.

And she . . . sucked at fighting mean.

At least she'd gotten better at hanging up.

That was progress—so long as her mom didn't call back.

Right on cue, her cell buzzed in her, and she nearly dropped it like it had suddenly caught fire. She would not pick up. She would not even glance at the screen.

Lie.

She looked, and saw,

*Can I tempt you with prickly pear margaritas?*

Frowning, the conversation with her mom tucking itself back into the box in the back of her heart with the countless others of that same vein, Heidi was trying to puzzle out who had her number and was texting her about margaritas—albeit delicious ones—when her cell vibrated again.

*Just realized you're probably wondering who this is. I'll give you one guess. It's your non-friend, who'd like to make up for Cake-Gate, and maybe a few more things.*

"Brad," she breathed.

Then immediately shook her head because she shouldn't be breathing dreamily about the man.

Another buzz as she was starting her car. Sighing, she couldn't stop herself from glancing at the screen before she backed out.

*I got your number from Kate.*

A beat.

*So she'll probably question why you'd refuse to see me when we're practically family now.*

"Brad," she growled, snatching up her cell from the cradle on her dash, fingers flying over the screen.

*So now you're not only good at slipping out unnoticed, but also blackmail?*

Another buzz.

*I'm exceptionally good at a lot of things.*

"Ugh," she muttered, shoving her cell into the bottom of her purse in disgust and then tossing her purse in the back seat for good measure.

Or maybe so she wouldn't be tempted to keep talking to the man.

Unfortunately, that was also true.

Regardless, she ignored the responding buzz and concentrated her attention on navigating her way through Bay Area traffic and home to her townhouse.

Which was the best thing she'd ever spent her money on.

Located in a small two-story building on the edge of town, it backed up to a lightly forested area. But her favorite part—besides the sauna inside the gym that she pretended to use but really it was just an excuse to make it into that sauna, and the fact that she had a quiet corner unit with a balcony looking out on those woods—were the trails crisscrossing through the trees, several of which led to a small creek. She could wander them for a few minutes, pretend that she was being healthy and was totally a nature girl, and when she'd had enough, be back inside her townhouse in fifteen minutes flat.

It was perfect.

But tonight, she wasn't finding that same satisfaction.

Because of her cell phone burning a hole in her purse.

"Self-respect," she murmured. "Self. Respect."

Except, her body didn't want self-respect. It wanted Brad and his yummy cock and for her to have a repeat of their night together—only this time minus the shitty morning-after feeling.

"That's it," she muttered, pulling out some ingredients for dinner and setting them on the counter. She would make pasta and bread and eat ice cream and drink wine. She would consume *all* the carbs, and then Brad would be gone, flitting from her life again as he traveled to some exotic location.

Heading into her bedroom with that thought, she spent the next few minutes changing from her fancy work clothes—fancy because of the meeting, since she normally wore jeans, T-shirts, and the odd blouse to her lab—into her coziest pajamas. She was tugging an oversized sweatshirt down her torso after hanging up her slacks and button-down, stowing away her sparkly flats, when her doorbell rang.

Smiling, she made her way to the door.

In all likelihood, it would be her neighbor, Mrs. Horowitz. The elderly widow usually came bearing delicious baked goods, and coincidentally, Heidi was out of banana chocolate chip muffins. Maybe she'd get enough of a carb stash to tide her over for a few days.

But when she tugged open the wooden panel, Mrs. Horowitz wasn't on the other side.

"Can I bribe my way inside?" Brad asked.

"No," she muttered, starting to slam the door.

"I have tequila," he coaxed.

"It's a school night." This time, she did shut the heavy wood, flicking the lock with a resounding *click*.

Then she heard the sigh.

A resolved one.

Like he'd known what her reaction was going to be, even before she'd opened and shut the door.

And she hesitated, guilt sliding through her to curl in her stomach. She didn't enjoy feeling like a bitch, especially when the man was probably lonely with his brother gone. He probably didn't have a lot of friends in town. She knew he'd only recently moved to California, that he worked from home, and his travels took him away frequently.

He didn't even have his family to hang out with.

They'd all returned home on Sunday.

So if she didn't take pity on the man, he would be all alone.

And lonely.

And sad.

Or maybe that was her?

Either way, she'd reopened the door.

But he wasn't there. The entry was empty, the street beyond quiet. She started to take a step forward, in an attempt to follow him when she couldn't begin to have a clue to know how to track him down or which way he'd left, and stopped.

Then glanced down and smiled despite herself.

There on her welcome mat was a basket, and inside it, a bottle of tequila, a bag of ice, a squirt bottle of prickly pear simple syrup, a shaker, and two glasses.

The man had charm—and balls—she had to give him that.

# SEVEN

Brad

*I'LL COOK. You mix. So long as you remember it's a school night.*

He glanced down at his cell and smiled.

Then got back out of his car, which he'd parked just down the block, and made his way to Heidi's door.

She was waiting in the opening, the rattiest sweatshirt he'd ever seen covering her lush curves, the basket he'd left in her arms. Her hair was down, her legs covered in rainbow-printed pajama pants, and her feet were bare, purple-painted toes peeking out from beneath the hem of her PJs.

And she was the most beautiful woman he'd ever seen.

Seeing her was an actual punch to the gut, a physical caress.

Then she spoke, and he'd be lying if he said it didn't take a tiny bit of wind out of his sails.

"I'm only inviting you in because you're alone."

Ouch.

But still, it was a way in. So he simply took the basket from her arms and said, "Well, if I'm here being pathetic, I don't mind being pathetic with you."

Her cheeks went pink. "That's not what I meant."

He knew that, knew despite the sharp words and her attempts at distance, that Heidi wasn't mean at heart. She had a generosity of spirit and a big heart, both of which had recalled him to her place, even after he'd clearly hurt her deeply a few months before.

Shifting the basket, he brushed his fingers over her cheek. "I know."

"No touching," she muttered, stepping back. "If you want my famous spaghetti Bolognese, you'll stop with the seduction and just be Jaime's brother."

He didn't want to be Jaime's brother in that moment.

He wanted to be this woman's lover, her other half, her everything.

But he'd blown it. He'd run scared last time, and now he was paying the consequences. Also yes, maybe he had a plan to sweet-talk this woman into a second chance. He'd fucked up, he panicked and left, but . . . he'd come back.

He'd *seen* her.

The puzzle pieces in his mind had finally rearranged themselves into proper alignment.

And he knew that he couldn't give her up.

Travel had grown dull, his life empty. But now he was seeing in full color for the first time, and that was simply from being in her presence for a few hours. He wanted more. He wanted *everything*.

He wanted . . . well, first he wanted this woman to not look at him with daggers in her eyes.

Baby steps.

Lifting his hands, he said, "No touching." A beat. "Unless you ask me to."

Her eyebrows lifted, and if her glare were a physical thing, he would have been flayed open and bleeding on the ground. As it was, and lucky for him, she didn't have that power, so he was able to follow her into the house, able to surreptitiously take in her surroundings.

To mark if anything had changed.

It hadn't, and he walked through the clean space, everything neatly in its place, from the dust-free photographs to the purple couch with the cheerful turquoise cushions. She strode into the kitchen, and he saw she had food set out on the counter. As he hovered in the doorway, she bent and grabbed a pot from a drawer, slamming more than placing it on the stove.

"Is there a reason you haven't started mixing drinks yet?" she muttered a little while later.

He'd been watching her at work, opening cans of tomato sauce, browning some meat in a pan—which had required her to do an additional bend and had given him an additional glimpse of those curves currently hiding amongst the rainbows on her pajamas—chopping an onion and herbs, and he hadn't realized that he'd spent long minutes standing in that opening.

She was mesmerizing.

Even grouchy and in enough fabric to cover an elephant.

Which was a thought he would not be saying aloud.

Because, once again, he liked his balls where they were, thank him very much.

"I thought it was a school night," he bluffed. "Figured you'd want to save your one drink for mealtime."

"I changed my mind," she muttered, stirring the pot after adding what smelled like garlic—and plenty of the yummy aromatic if his nose was any indication. "I need more than one drink to deal with you creeping out on me like a peeping Tom."

He burst out laughing.

"That wasn't supposed to be funny."

Crossing over to her, he said, "You're like a kitten trying to be terrifying, hissing and swiping out with your claws but not managing anything remotely close to frightening."

Her hazel eyes darkened.

And he had the distinct thought that if he *really* liked his balls where they currently resided, then he was going to have to stop running his freaking mouth.

But instead of taking her frustration out on his junk, instead of smacking him over the head with that pan—as he probably half-deserved—her lips curved into a rueful smile and she said, "Unfortunately, I've never mastered the art of being scary."

"That's not so bad."

"Oh yeah?" she muttered. "You haven't seen me trying to scare off annoying men in the bar. One of my glares and I swear they pull up a chair and start ordering appetizers." She turned back to the sauce and stirred in one of the cans of tomatoes.

"I'm guessing it doesn't work on annoying men in your house, either?"

Her lips tipped up. "No, it doesn't."

He laughed, finally placed the basket on the counter, started pulling together ingredients for the prickly pear margaritas that he'd heard through the grapevine were her favorite.

"I'm not good at seeing things through to the end." Brad froze, shocked that he'd said the words aloud.

He'd thought them often enough, had berated himself for his jumping about, for his lack of staying power, but he couldn't ever remember a time when he'd admitted that failing to someone else.

She didn't say anything for a long moment, the silence punctuated only by the sizzling meat in the pan, the scraping of the wooden spoon as she stirred.

"Why do you think that is?" she asked softly, when he'd

nearly given in to the urge to run screaming from the townhouse.

The question was an obvious one.

Just not one he'd expected her to ask.

It was also one he wasn't prepared to answer.

"I don't know." Did it relate to his mom? Was it some other failing? Some defense mechanism? Maybe they were all tied together . . . or maybe he was just flawed.

Maybe he had more thinking to do.

*Sigh.*

She turned, gave him that glare again, the one that was supposed to be scary but was really freaking adorable, and said, "You think I'm going to let you off the hook that easily?"

No, of course she wasn't.

But before his discussion with Jaime, he'd never talked to anyone about this, had never done more than laugh off the comments when people—from teachers to family members to friends—teased him about his flights of fancy and his tendency to go off on his own adventures. Even his career had been something he'd fallen into—website design, predominately for travel companies. His first client had reached out to him after finding Brad's now-retired travel blog.

See what he meant about not finishing things?

But truthfully, with the blog at least, he'd gotten too busy with his website business, with all the places he'd traveled, to keep up. It was either turn down clients or travel less or let the blog go.

The decision had been easy.

Buh-bye blog.

But how to explain that to this woman.

"Okay, fine," she said, after a moment. "Maybe I *will* let you off that easily."

He snorted.

"Be prepared for me to circle back after prickly pears."

"Noted."

She smiled at him and turned back to the pan. "What's your favorite place you've visited?"

He measured the alcohol into the metal cup, scooped up some ice, shook the entire mixture together, and then strained it into two glasses. "We're going to be friends now?"

"I've decided to forgive you."

His heart pulsed. "Just that easily?"

"I've punished you for two days straight, not to mention laughed when you got brained by that platter." He touched the top of his head, probing the still painful spot, and she laughed. "See? I'm terrible."

No, she was wonderful.

Especially when her eyes narrowed. "But I am *not* sleeping with you again."

Now, it was his turn to laugh.

She crossed to him, making his breath catch, his laughter cut off. And his cock twitch. Like it did any time she was in the vicinity. "I am," she murmured, her mouth temptingly close, her floral and spice scent wafting up into his nose. "*Not* sleeping with you again," she added, reaching beyond him for the glass he'd just filled then retreating back across the kitchen.

"Why?" he asked. "You know it would be good."

She'd just taken a sip—or maybe, a gulp. Either way, his assertion made her sputter and cough, and then *he* crossed to *her*, rubbing his hand up and down her spine until she stopped choking, until she looked up at him, heat in her eyes.

Her breath shuttered out. "I'm still not sleeping with you," she wheezed.

Their gazes met.

They both burst into laughter.

And Brad thought that was okay. For now, anyway.

Baby steps.

First laughter.

Then, hopefully, other things.

# EIGHT

Heidi

IT WAS THE NEXT EVENING, and she was having *déjà vu*.

"Glutton for punishment?" she asked, lifting her brows at the tall, dark, and sexy pain in her ass currently sitting on her doorstep.

He lifted his cell. "You didn't text me to stay away, so I figured that I'd slide into the chance."

Snorting, she unlocked her door, moving inside and allowing him to trail her down the hall. "The ignoring was unintentional. My cell had to be off for my work today"—some top-secret shit, as her assistant Stef called it—"and I forgot to turn it on." She plunked the box with the muffins she'd picked up after work and her bag on the kitchen counter, reached inside, and pulled her phone out. "See? It's not all about you."

He smiled that slow and hot quirk of his lips, making her want to ignore her promise to herself.

But she was stubborn.

She wouldn't be burned twice by falling for his humor and charm.

Even if he was humorous . . . and charming.

Friends, and nothing more. That. Was. *It.*

He snagged the cell from her fingers and powered it on. "But seriously, don't forget, next time," he said, tone more serious than she had ever heard it. "You might get into a situation where you need it and can't wait for it to boot up."

She paused. "Have *you* been in one of those situations?"

Humor in his gorgeous green-brown eyes, tempering the serious. "More than one."

"Oh."

"Yeah. *Oh.*" He handed her phone back.

Heidi took it and found herself hesitant, all of a sudden remembering that him coming over to hang out, especially unexpectedly, wasn't normal. Yes, they'd eaten together the previous night. Yes, they'd chatted a bit about the places he'd visited. Yes, she'd actually had three prickly pear margaritas. But then she'd yawned, right in the middle of him telling her a story about a pickpocket he'd fended off in Italy, and he hadn't finished his tale, hadn't listened to her when she'd told him she was fine.

Nope. He'd shown himself right to the door.

And she hadn't heard a word from him.

She'd just slept, worked, and expected to go on with their separate lives—his guilt assuaged, her life moving right along. She even had plans tonight to set up an online dating profile for a new app Stef had recommended.

Apparently, all the cool kids were doing it.

Not that *she* was a cool kid, but it wasn't like she had anything to lose. Plus, maybe she'd find someone who stuck around.

"You'll keep it on?" he asked. Or well, it *sounded* like a question, but his gaze suggested it was more of an order.

*All* order.

And she shivered, heat pooling between her thighs at the

memory of his previous commands, of the pleasure they had found together, of the husky voice, the hard cock, the talented fingers driving her to orgasm as he'd spent the night ordering her around.

*Legs around my waist.*

*Give me your mouth.*

*Come for me. Now, baby.*

Sex. Just sex.

And she wanted more. But unfortunately—no, not *unfortunately*. Not having more of Brad was a good thing. Self-respect and loving herself and understanding she needed more were all good things.

*Orgasms are good things,* her inner devil prodded.

But she wasn't going there. Couldn't—

*Me thinks you doth protest too much.*

Ugh!

Ignoring her mental quarreling, she straightened her shoulders and lifted a brow. "Not sure why that sounds like an order."

He grinned. "Probably because it is one."

Glaring, though she couldn't deny that part of her was amused, she hung her purse on the hook she'd installed by the door for just that purpose, stepped out of her shoes, and tucked them neatly on the rack in the hall. Organization was her life's blood—well, organization along with *Twilight*, but she wasn't about to admit *that* guilty pleasure to the world.

It was only bearable that Cora, Kate, and Kelsey knew her innermost secret because she knew her friends' own guilty pleasures, too—unicorns, Hermione Granger, and being freakishly smart, so much so that she collected post-graduate degrees for *fun*, respectively. Still, organization was a perfectly acceptable guilty pleasure for a woman of her age (even though she was still Team Edward the whole way), and it was easier to focus on hooks and folders and perfectly dusted shelves than on blood-sucking, teenage love, and immortal life.

Though, just thinking about it, and she was jonesing for a reread.

"Want another order?" he asked. "I'm sure I can rustle one up. Don't walk alone in the dark. Always check the back seat of your car before you get in."

She'd been so focused on her *Twilight* and organizational haze that she'd forgotten they were having a conversation, particularly a conversation about orders.

She rolled her eyes. "First, those are all examples of the patriarchal bullshit in our society. Women should be able to walk safely any time of day or night and not have to worry about a man accosting them. Or lying in wait in their car. Along that vein, men should also be taught to respect women and their autonomy, and it's such horseshit that women are always told to walk in groups and not to leave their drinks unattended and—"

"You're right," he said. "It *is* bullshit."

Her lips parted on an exhale.

"*Of course* it's total bullshit that those are things you have to consider—or are *told* to consider as a woman." A beat, his hazel eyes dimming. "But unfortunately, just because we *think* that things should be different, doesn't mean they are."

He had a point there.

She still didn't have to like it. "Maybe," she muttered. "But I'm still a grown woman, and there's not a chance in hell that I'll obey any orders you give, just because you give them."

His brows pulled together, those hazel eyes flashing, becoming more brown than green. "You'd risk your life to prove a point?"

"Of course not," she said. "But I'm an adult who makes her own choices."

End of story.

He was still, his shoulders stiff, his jaw clenched, but then abruptly that whole demeanor faded, and he relaxed, mouth turned up at the corner. "Are we having our first fight?"

"More like tenth," she muttered, moving to the fridge. "I suppose you're staying for dinner." A beat as she glanced back at him. "As fr—"

"Friends," he finished for her. Then smiled again. "So long as you're good to cook for me again."

She'd already begun pulling out ingredients for a salad. "Is this your strategy when you're home? Bum food off whatever stranger will take you in?"

"When the stranger is a beautiful woman who's not actually a stranger, and who just happens to be an excellent cook, great company, and sexy as hell?" He grinned. "Yup."

"Careful," she warned.

"I'm not lying."

"Just spinning bullshit."

"Not at this moment," he said. "That may affect my ability to get some of your delicious food."

"Maybe I'll use the opportunity to poison you."

He snorted. "I have no allergies."

"Allergies aren't poison."

"Conveniently, I have spent many years building up my resistance to all types of poison."

"*A la Princess Bride?*"

"Exactly."

She grinned, despite herself. "Well, you have good taste because it's my second favorite movie."

"Seriously?"

"Seriously."

"Only *second* favorite?"

Heidi giggled.

"At any rate, I'll take it because you should see *this*." It was said with such flourish that she glanced up from where she was chopping veggies to watch him pull out a DVD from the bag he carried. It was a copy of *Princess Bride*. "We're soul mates."

She giggled. "You're ridiculous."

"No," he deadpanned. "I'm Brad Huntington. And you've crushed my ego. Prepare to . . ." He screwed up his face. "Dine?"

More giggles bubbled up in her chest. "I stand by my previous statement. Ridiculous."

"What can I say? I nerd out about Rob Reiner films. Well, him and Billy Crystal."

"Hmm."

He crossed over to her, leaned a hip to the counter. "Hmm, what?"

"Hmm as in, okay, maybe we *can* be friends," she said.

He tilted his head to the side, studying her. "Because I'm a nerd?"

"Because the *only* things I respect are nerds. Case in point"—she pointed at her chest—"nerd."

A shrug. "Well, I'll take my victory in any avenue possible."

"Whatever makes you feel better." She turned back to the fridge and grabbed some chicken, belatedly realizing that a man as big as Brad probably wouldn't be filled up by a salad. "What else did you bring?"

"Besides the most glorious movie of all time, you mean?" he asked.

"The *second* most glorious movie," she countered. "And yes."

He reached into the bag and pulled out a pint of ice cream. "I heard somewhere once that women like chocolate . . . and ice cream."

"Except me." She shook her head. "I can't stand sweet things." Never mind that she'd pounded three pieces of the replacement cake at Kate's wedding the weekend before—both because she had missed the dinner portion of festivities with her cake shenanigans and attempts at saving it, and because . . . she had a sweet tooth.

A major sweet tooth.

His face fell, and immediately she felt guilty that her joke didn't land.

"I'm kidding," she quickly said. "Given the chance, I would make love to that ice cream all night long."

Face clearing, he said, "And here I am, friend-zoned, so I can't partake in the festivities." He stashed the ice cream in the freezer. "I'll just go set up the DVD?"

Except . . .

"About that," she began.

"Oh, you don't want to watch it? We don't have to watch anything. I just thought—" A shake of his head. "I just thought that you might want to . . ." He trailed off, reached into his bag. "I brought a game, too. In case—"

Her heart squeezed.

"I do want to watch it," she told him. "I just don't have a DVD player."

He froze. "You don't *have* a DVD player? I travel the world for half the year, and *I* have one in my tiny, postage stamp of an apartment."

"I don't have one," she confirmed. "But unlike the old man currently taking up space in my kitchen, I *do* have the digital copy, which means that I don't need to have a DVD player." She smiled smugly. "I can stream it on *all* my devices."

His incredulity had faded as she spoke, and he drifted closer. "*All* your devices." He waggled his brows. "And yes, the innuendo was intended."

She sniffed. "You're as bad as the girls with your dirty jokes."

"Hmm." He shifted closer. "I like it when you say *dirty*."

Placing a hand on his chest, she shoved him away so she could grab a pan to cook the chicken. "Ugh. I'm still not—"

"Going to sleep with me." He lightly tugged a lock of her hair. "I've got that."

"And yet, you're still here," she whispered.

He froze.

*She* froze.

Steady hazel eyes on hers. "Do you want me to go?"

Three days ago at the wedding she would have said yes, and she would have meant it, too. At least with . . . say ninety-five percent of her being. The other five percent was still wrapped up in the yummy hormones and delicious orgasms. But after the night of the wedding, after *last* night, she—and yes, she was fully aware that this was probably exceptionally stupid—but she didn't want him to go.

She wanted to watch the movie with him, to listen to him tell her about his travel adventures.

She wanted to spend more time with this man.

As a friend.

*Only* as a friend.

Except, that line was getting more difficult for her to convince herself of, especially the more time she spent with Brad.

Luckily for her, she could occasionally manage to ostrich with the best of them. Because tonight was all about avoiding the traitorous and dangerous thoughts in her mind and sticking her head in the proverbial sand. She would continue pretending she only liked his company as a friend and was hanging out with him just because she missed Kate.

Obviously, she had to fill that space with someone. Brad was as good a fit as anyone.

See? Ostrich.

She could be good at it.

Either way, her mental sand-head-sticking worked. She was able to turn to him, to lift her lips in a smile.

"No," she whispered.

His eyes met hers, held. "Okay. I'll stay."

She turned back to the pan, heart pounding, only to whip back around a minute later when he began trying to tempt her away from the movie. "Oh no, you don't," she ordered, interrupting his expounding on the merits of the board game he'd brought. "You don't get to tease by taking away *Princess Bride* after you offered it to me."

He stopped talking, then his eyes darkened, lips quirking. "Teasing?"

She smacked him lightly with a spoon. "No more innuendos." A beat. "Now make yourself useful and cut up that cucumber."

Mischief crept across his face.

She smacked him again.

Then they both gave in and started laughing.

God, she loved laughing with this man.

# NINE

Brad

SHE'D FALLEN asleep right around the time Fezzik says, "Anyone want a peanut?"

Slumping back against the cushions, her lips parted on slow and steady breaths.

He watched her through the duel, through the hillside tumble, through the castle storming scene, and then he forced himself to get up, to quietly take care of the dishes, and pack away the leftovers. By then, the movie was over, so he scooped her up and carried her into the bedroom.

Settling her under the covers only took a moment, but the temptation to stay, to crawl in next to her, was strong.

Except, she'd made it clear what her boundaries were.

And he wasn't enough of an asshole to barrel his way past them.

After tucking the blanket around her, he smoothed her hair back from her face, smiling when her eyebrows drew together into a slight frown. Then he stepped back.

He'd save the crawling-in-beside-her for a future date.

Until then, he turned for the door, saw something—well, *two* somethings on the shelf beside it that had him pausing, considering, and then grinning again.

He snagged them both.

One went into his pocket.

The other he paired with a pen and did what he should have done after that first night.

He left Heidi a note.

*Then* he let himself out of the apartment.

---

EVEN WHEN HE wasn't halfway around the world, he still couldn't stand staying in one place for long.

Luckily, the Bay Area had no shortage of beautiful places to visit.

And he was like a kid in the candy store, trying to visit each and every one of them.

He'd worked until the sky had just begun to lighten, putting the finishing touches on a website for an up-and-coming airline. Then he'd gotten into his car and driven north along the coast.

Over the Golden Gate, spending more time in traffic than he preferred, but once he'd made it away from the commuters, his journey up the winding highway had been quiet.

After parking along one edge of the road, his car tucked onto a narrow strip of gravel, he climbed out from behind the wheel, navigated the rickety wooden stairs that led down to the beach, and sat on a washed-up log to watch the sky grow bright, filtering in through the heavy fog, gilding the area in an almost-otherworldly glow.

He was just standing, ready to find his feet, to drive back to his apartment and sleep when his cell vibrated.

Retrieving it from his pocket, he saw that Heidi was calling him.

Not texting.

But actually calling him.

A call he was going to miss if he didn't actually swipe his finger across the screen and answer it.

"Hello?" he said, getting his shit together and lifting it up to his ear.

"And they say an old dog doesn't learn new tricks," Heidi said on a laugh that sent heat trickling down his spine, his cock twitching in remembrance of what that laugh had felt like on his skin.

She'd gotten his note.

His lips curved up, happiness sliding through him. "You calling me a dog?"

Another laugh. "I most certainly am."

"Well, this one *has* learned new tricks."

"I see that." She paused. "Thanks for last night."

"You did the cooking."

"And you brought the ice cream," she said. "In my book, that's more than half the battle."

"So, the key to your heart is through ice cream."

A husky chuckle that had him wishing all over again he'd stayed that night, that he'd left a note that first time, that he hadn't been a fucking coward when he'd recognized this woman was someone he should be staying for.

"Not exactly," she said. "The key to my heart is . . ." She trailed off, and he could see her smile in his mind. It would be tinged with a smirk, one corner of her mouth curved higher than the other, and her hazel eyes—the mix of gold and green—would be dancing with humor. "No," she said. "I'm going to leave that for you to figure out."

Every cell in his body froze, jumping to absolute, rigid attention.

Was she saying . . .

Was he getting another chance?

"Heidi—"

A sea gull cawed loudly over his head.

"Where are you?"

He waited for the bird to quiet before saying, "The beach."

Silence. Then. "Of course, you are."

"What does that mean?"

"Only that *only* you would be absconding to the beach on a Thursday morning when most people are commuting to work." She laughed. "Are you ever not the wayward traveler?"

Yes.

When he was with *her*.

When he spent time with Heidi, he didn't think about the ever-growing list of places he wanted to visit. And when he was with her, he certainly didn't imagine traveling alone. He pictured her with him, going to all the cliché places, her hair flowing through the breeze as they walked along the canals of Venice, kissing her under the Eiffel Tower, holding her hand as they circled the upright rocks of Stonehenge. And more. He imagined her on a trek in South America, winding through colorful plateaus, on a hike through trees so tall it was nearly impossible to see the tops. He wondered if she'd go cave-diving with him, spelunking through tunnels in New Zealand, searching for glowworms. He'd bet he could convince her to visit a castle on the coast of Northern Ireland.

"Brad?"

He blinked, forced himself to focus on the conversation rather than the fantasies in his brain. "I'm here. And yes, there are times when I want to do nothing more than sleep in my own bed."

"So, why do you travel so much?" she asked, her tone not unkind. Rather, it was laced with curiosity and softness.

Sighing, he stared out at the horizon, now bright with pops of pink and orange and deep blue peeking out through the fog. "I . . ." He stopped himself from giving her the same pat answer he always gave everyone—that he didn't want to settle down, that there was so much world to explore, and he didn't want to miss an inch of it.

All of that was true, of course.

But as he'd come to realize, there was also something more.

"I guess it's just always been expected that I was the one who'd run wild."

A beat of quiet. Then a soft question. "Why was it expected?"

The log was getting uncomfortable under his ass, but this woman was in his head and heart, and he knew he'd answer anything she asked. "Tammy was always the smart sibling, so it's no surprise she's spent most of her adult life in school. Though she has her second master's in business administration now and is looking to take the corporate world by storm."

"I met her at the wedding." Heidi chuckled. "And I'm definitely not surprised to hear that in the least. I have no doubt she'll succeed. What about Jaime and Penny?"

"Jaime has always been the caring one, so it's no surprise he ended up as a vet. And Penny is the second oldest, even though she pretends otherwise." He smiled. "Mostly because she's made an art form out of ordering everyone around."

"Doesn't she run her own business?"

"Yup. One that just went public a couple of weeks ago and is killing it in its valuations."

His siblings would probably be surprised to know that he'd followed each of their lives so closely. He knew they thought of him as being so wrapped up in his own life and his adventures that he didn't have time for anyone else. But he'd always made it home for the important stuff—birthdays, weddings, Christmas, his parents' anniversary. He loved his family, even more than he loved traveling. Which was why he followed his brother's vet practice on Instagram, why he'd made it home for all three of Tammy's college graduations, why he'd been there to watch Penny ring the bell on Wall Street when her company went public.

Traveling was his life's blood.

But he only left because he knew he had something solid to come home to.

"And what about you?" Heidi asked. "Which one are you?"

That was the trouble, wasn't it?

He didn't really know.

"My mom always called me her little explorer," he said. "From the time I was little, I was climbing trees and trying to run off in parking lots. We took a trip to London once when I was a kid, and she always says that was the one time I actually stayed by her side." He laughed. "Because I was too busy looking around to wander off. I remember the trip, and it's true. I thought it was amazing and so different from the little Midwest town we grew up in. Then I studied abroad my junior year in college and fed the travel bug that had bit me by traveling all over Europe."

"And you haven't stopped?"

"No," he said. "I haven't stopped. I work for two things—well, three things, I suppose. One, retirement. Two, to eat. Three, to travel."

"So, why did you move out here? It's got to be more expensive keeping an apartment in the Bay Area than where you used to live."

That was true.

"When my parents followed Tammy and Jaime out here, I

figured it was better to have a place close to everyone." Even though Penny was still in the Midwest, she was thinking of moving to this coast, since increasingly more of her business was keeping her in San Francisco.

It was a Huntington invasion.

"That's sweet."

He shrugged, even though she couldn't see him. "It just made sense. What about you?" he added. "How long have you been in California?"

"Born and raised." A chuckle. "East Bay all the way."

"And you haven't gone far."

"Nope. Just away to college and then right back here." She laughed. "Hang on a second." There was a blip of noise, almost sounding like she'd rolled her window down, and then he heard her say, "Thanks." He waited another moment, and then her voice was back on the line. "Sorry about that."

"Where are you?"

"Driving into work. I had to show my credentials," she said, tone amused. "As my assistant would say, so I don't put the top-secret shit at risk."

"Top-secret? Wow, color me impressed."

She snorted. "It's a lot less exciting than it sounds. Trust me. I'm just a nerd with lots of computers, running lots of models, who spends her days in muffin-crumb-covered T-shirts and chugs coffee like it's my life's blood."

"What's your favorite type of muffin?"

"Banana chocolate chip. From Molly's." She waited a beat. "What's yours?"

"I don't know, cinnamon and sugar?" *He* waited a beat. "What's Molly's?"

"*What's* Molly's?" She gasped. "Only the best bakery in all of the Bay Area. And as a connoisseur of all things baked goods, *that's* saying something."

"I guess I'll have to check out this Molly's."

"Not without me," Heidi said. "It's sacrilege to go by yourself the first time. You need help navigating the deliciousness."

"Deliciousness?" He couldn't help but tease. "Is that even a word?"

"Don't know," she said, her voice going slightly muffled. "Don't care. Unless that caring gets me to Molly's."

"Is this you asking me on a date?"

"Again," she said. "Don't care, so long as it gets me to Molly's sooner."

He laughed outright. "You'll take me to Molly's as soon as possible."

"Sold." A beat. "You coming over tonight?"

His heart squeezed tight, excitement trickling through him. She was asking him over. She'd *called* him. This was big. This was him making his way back into her good graces. This was him getting his second chance. "Do you *want* me to come over?"

"I . . . well . . ." Now there was hesitation in her words. *Shit.* He should have just said yes.

"Heidi—"

Voices in the background.

"I've got to go." He heard a rustling, as though she'd lifted the phone from her ear.

"Heidi," he said quickly, pulse pounding in his veins.

The rustling stopped. "Yeah?"

"I'll bring pizza."

Silence. Long, interminable silence.

Then a soft sigh. "I'll be home by six."

Relief poured through him as they said goodbye and hung up. God, he was so not smooth, so not a player. He'd already fucked up the best thing he'd ever had with a woman once. Now he needed to be smart, to play this right.

Because Heidi was . . . everything.

# TEN

Heidi

NORMALLY, her work drew her in, made her lose all sense of time, forget every bit of her real life.

Normally, she was reduced to spreadsheets and calculations, the occasional coffee and muffin break. Oh, and her favorite kind of email exchange.

With her dad.

He wasn't like her mom. He was nice, if more than a bit absentminded and wrapped up in whatever project he was currently working on. She remembered that distance used to hurt her feelings. But then he'd seemed to sense her loneliness, or maybe some part of him had finally registered what her mom's sharp words had been doing, because one day he had brought her to his lab.

He hadn't said a word to her mother.

Just packed her up one Saturday morning, loading her backpack with coloring materials, books, her favorite set of paper dolls—she'd had a thing for the American Girl dolls when she was young, okay?—and plenty of snacks, and they had disappeared into the world of science for a day.

She'd fallen out of love with paper dolls.

And into love with mass spectrometry.

Yup, the nerd gene ran deep.

Her mom had been furious—she'd missed some activity that Colleen had deemed *very* important for Heidi's female education, never mind that she'd been all of seven at the time—but that hadn't stopped her dad from taking her back every Saturday.

And sometimes on Sundays, too.

That time had kept her sane.

She still didn't understand how her dad could be married to her mom—it wasn't like she didn't love her mom. She was her mom; *of course* Heidi loved her.

She just . . . didn't like her.

But she loved her dad, and she kept in regular email contact with him, and because of him, she'd held on to her sanity during her childhood. Also, she supposed her mom wasn't *always* completely awful. Occasionally Colleen said something nice, and it wasn't like her entire childhood had been traumatic.

There had been good times.

They just . . . mostly involved her dad.

But regardless of the good or bad times, she loved that she could boot up her computer, get to work, and start the day with an email from her dad,

*Remind me of the assay calculation for barrelene we talked about last time?*

She loved that she could smile over lunch at the picture he'd sent of him posing in front of his new mass spectrometer.

And then feel her heart squeeze with happiness when he sent mid-afternoon,

*I read your paper. It's good, peanut. I'm proud of you.*

Silly, huh?

Short little notes in her dad's typical scattershot method. Some days they'd exchange two dozen emails, sometimes a week would go by without a word. But their virtual contact would always pick right back up as though they were in the middle of a conversation. It was never uncomfortable, never strained.

Just . . . connection.

And like it had been when she was a kid, that connection was over science. Luckily, she loved both her dad *and* the theoretical properties of barrelene, even if it was a long ways from the molecular physics she studied and used in her lab.

Signing off on her reply to the final email, an exchange that would normally energize her for several more hours, Heidi found her eyes going back to the clock.

Again.

Counting the minutes down until she could leave. Again.

Because despite the emails from her dad, for the first day ever, she hated her job.

Part of her kept repeating the conversation from that morning back to her, cringing at the desperate way she'd asked Brad to come over. Brad, who she wasn't going to see as a love interest. Brad, who she wasn't going to sleep with. Brad, who she was only going to be friends with.

And Brad . . . who she wanted to be so much more than that.

Sighing, she tapped a few keys across her keyboard, logged off her computer, and pushed back from her desk. "I'm out of here," she told Stef.

"Everything okay?" her assistant asked.

"Fine. Just my brain is fried. I'm going to call it a day."

Stef nodded, and they spent a couple of minutes discussing the day's outstanding items. Fifteen minutes later, she was signing out of the lab and heading toward her car.

Then she was on her way home, ridiculously early.

But she honestly couldn't hate the ridiculously early, not when it was smooth sailing through traffic, not when she took fifteen minutes upon arriving to her complex to bypass her condo and walk down her little trail. She stood in front of the little creek, trying to get the fist gripping her heart to relax—the same fist that was telling her to run from Brad, that she'd only get hurt again.

Because she *had* been hurt.

Deeply.

After one night.

Which was . . . too much and ridiculous and something that shouldn't have been possible. She'd slept with plenty of people, so Brad being a one-off shouldn't have hurt.

Except, his leaving without a word had.

And now, she worried that she would be opening herself up for a *world* of that hurt if she let him back in, if she *dove* into things with him, like she so desperately wanted. They'd had all of one phone conversation. Had only spent a couple of hours together. He'd left a note. Not poetry. Not undying love. Not . . . *what?*

What was she looking for?

She had no freaking clue.

Aside from the fact that all of those things were combining to draw her more firmly down the rabbit hole that was Brad Huntington.

Could she risk being his friend without falling in deep?

Because he would inevitably leave, and he would leave her behind.

But . . . what if he wanted her to come along?

"This is pointless," she muttered to the tiny babbling creek. "We slept together. We hung out a bit. That's it. It's not life-changing, even if it feels like it."

And it *did* feel like it. She was addicted.

She wanted more.

But he was going to leave.

It was an inevitability.

"So, knowing that," she whispered, "why can't I just enjoy the process? Why can't I just go in and have fun and soak in every bit of the experience?" She tossed a rock into the water. "Because, dumbass, you've been talking a big talk about wanting more, about wanting something more than just a quick fuck." A sigh. "And you'll never have that with Brad."

"I don't want a quick fuck."

Heidi shrieked and spun around, losing her footing at the sound of the voice so very close to her ear. She slid down the embankment, dirt and leaves rolling over her, landing in a heap at the bottom, the all of three inches of water in the creek soaking into her jeans.

"Heidi!"

A second later, Brad was at her side, scooping her up, holding her tightly against him.

"I'm fine," she said, shaking her head to clear it. "You can put me down."

"I didn't mean to scare you," he muttered, definitely *not* putting her down as he carried her up the slope, back onto solid ground.

"I'm all wet. Put me down before you get soaked, too," she said.

Scorching hazel eyes on hers had her replaying her words.

"That wasn't an innuendo," she muttered.

Those eyes narrowed, and she realized that the heat in his

gaze wasn't remotely sexual. No, instead, it was fury. Pissed-off, intense anger.

"I never expected it to be," he snapped.

"Why are you mad?" she asked, putting aside her request to be put down.

He bent down and snagged her purse. "I hurt you."

"I'm not hurt," she said. "I'm fine."

His eyes flashed to hers again, and as he started carrying her back down the trail, she placed her hand on his chest.

"I swear, Brad. I'm not hurt." Her groin might be a little tetchy from the slip-slide—she must have been attempting to do the splits while falling down that ridiculously tiny hill—but she was fine.

"You're bleeding."

Her mouth fell. "What?"

"You're bleeding."

"I can't be bl—"

He stopped, spinning them, and in a heartbeat, he had her pinned between his chest and a tree trunk, her purse crammed into her abdomen. One hand lifted, brushed lightly against the top of her cheek. He held it up so she could see the bright red painting his fingertips. "You're bleeding."

Her heart stuttered. "Just a little."

Eyes flashing again. He was fierce, glaring down at her, with the setting sun gathering in the trees, shafts of sunlight highlighting motes of dust in the air, the wind lightly rustling through the leaves. "A. Little?"

The last was said so dangerously that she shivered, heat trickling down her torso, gathering in her stomach, making her thighs tremble.

In a second, his expression shifted. "You're cold." He shifted again, straightening and cradling her against his chest, and starting to walk along the path again. "I need to get you inside and warm."

Heidi found herself without words.

She'd not expected him to be like this, to be so intense, so ferocious in his protection of her.

It was . . . not numbing exactly, but she was suddenly having an out-of-body experience as he carried her along her little trail, his legs eating up the space in hardly any time at all. What had taken her fifteen minutes of meandering, took him just a handful, and when he was walking up the stairs to her door, holding her like she weighed no more than a feather, she still hadn't found her voice.

All she could think was . . . she hadn't expected this.

Probably, that said bad things about her and her intelligence —that being held by this man had fried her brain—but she was still struggling to reconcile the normally easy-going, funny man with this one in front of her.

Though, he *had* gotten all protective about her phone.

"Keys," he said, stopping in front of her door.

She blinked. "What?"

His jaw clenched, a muscle twitching in the hard line, tempting her with a desire to taste that little pulsing spot, to soothe away the tension. But she didn't have a chance. He wedged her against the door, dug her keys out of her purse, then somehow managed to finagle them into the lock to open it.

A moment later, they were inside.

He kicked it shut and carried her down the hall, dumping her onto her bed. "Stay," he growled and then disappeared out of the room.

She stood up, not wanting to get her blankets wet, and moved to her dresser, opening the top drawer to pull out some pajamas.

Which was the moment Brad came back into the bedroom.

His eyes met hers in the mirror. "What part of *stay* don't you understand?"

Fresh pair of underwear in her grip, she dropped her hands to her side. "Are you fucking serious right now?"

His expression turned mulish.

"What part of stay don't I *understand?*" She spun to face him, crossing the room and prodding him the chest with her finger. "*S*tay? Fucking *stay?*"

He captured her finger. "You're bleeding. You're limping. I reserve the right to go a little crazy."

"You don't have *any* rights. Reserved or not. Bleeding and limping or not." Even *if* her cheek was starting to burn, and her groin, along with her ankle, *were* feeling a bit sore. She whirled around, took a step—

And stumbled.

Brad caught her. "Woman," he muttered.

Then she was in his arms again, pressed against his chest, his heat surrounding her, his scent in her nose. He marched into the bathroom, set her on the counter, and then turned to crank on the shower.

Her breath hitched when she saw the look on his face, fury written into every line, but his fingers were gentle when he reached for the hem of her T-shirt and tugged it over her head, when he unfastened the button on her jeans and slid down the zipper before hefting her again and working the damp material down her legs. He started to set her down then hesitated, reaching for a towel and tucking it beneath her before setting her on the marble surface.

The small act of kindness, the bit of care without a word undid her.

"Brad," she whispered.

His eyes came to hers, filled with an emotion that made her lose her breath all over again. "I can't hurt you again," he whispered. "I did it once. I can't be responsible for doing it again."

Her heart rolled over in her chest. "I'm not hurt."

He didn't answer, instead reaching for a small towel, dampening it in the sink, and bringing it up to her cheek, dabbing lightly at the cut.

She inhaled sharply, the sting taking her by surprise.

"You're hurt," he whispered.

She covered her hand with his. "It's just a little cut."

He set the towel aside, stepped away to check the shower temperature. Then he stripped off his shirt, shoved his pants down, and scooped her up again.

"What are you—?"

He stepped into the shower with her.

Hot water sluiced over her skin, soaking into her bra and underwear, slicking their skin, and suddenly, she didn't feel the cut, or her aching groin, or the slight throb in her ankle. She could only feel Brad. Just the wide breadth of his chest, the strength of his arms, the abrasion of the damp lace of her bra against her nipples, the cotton growing hot and wet between her thighs.

"Better?" he asked.

And she had to remember how to speak again.

Because this was a hell of a lot better. It was fucking incredible and not enough. It was intoxicating, and she was desperate for more. It was—

"Put me down," she whispered.

His gaze met hers, and whatever he saw there must have been intense enough that he actually listened to her, setting her carefully on her feet.

"Why are you doing this?" she asked, voice barely above a murmur.

His eyes slid closed, opened slowly, then his hand came up,

cupping her uninjured cheek gently. "I've spent the last months hating myself for leaving that night." His shoulders rose and fell on a breath. "Because it was more."

More. More. *More.*

The word echoed through her mind.

"I didn't know what I felt that night—" A sharp shake of his head. "No, that's a fucking lie, and I promised myself I wouldn't lie to you, not after I'd seen what it did to you when I treated you like that." His fingers convulsed slightly. "You're a fucking keeper, Heidi. You're the real deal—smart, beautiful, funny, kind—and I wanted to keep you from the first moment I laid eyes on you." He slid his hand to her nape. "Then we made love. Then I got to hold and touch you, to be inside you . . . and I knew I'd give up *everything* for a shot with you."

Her heart thudded against her ribs—a rapid *whoosh-whoosh, whoosh-whoosh, whoosh-whoosh.* Water streamed down her skin, warm rivulets that slid down her back, her legs, dripped forward and over her breasts.

"But you knew you couldn't actually give everything up," she whispered.

His face sobered. "No, I couldn't." A moment of quiet as she felt like she'd been stabbed in the gut.

Pretty words.

Nice compliments.

But he still hadn't wanted to stay.

God, here she was wanting him so much that she was almost willing to sacrifice her beliefs, to ignore everything she'd promised to jump into bed with him again. "I need you to go," she whispered.

"Heidi."

"You need to go," she repeated. "You need to *go.*"

"I—"

"*You need to go!*"

He retreated a step then his face clouded. "*No*," he said. "Not until you understand. Yes, I fucking panicked. Yes, I ran off that night because you made me feel things I have never felt with anyone. Yes, I left because it was too fucking much!" She flinched. "But I've thought about you every fucking day since then. I dreamed about you. I imagined what it would be like to have you with me."

Her chest rose and fell rapidly, her pulse danced a speedy tattoo in her veins. She couldn't summon any words, but it didn't matter.

Because he kept talking.

"Yes, I ran, but I've regretted it every day since." He closed the distance between them. "All I've wanted to do, all I *want* to do is make it up to you."

Her air stuttered out. "Brad."

His hand came up to her uninjured cheek again. "So, maybe I'm fucking this up. Maybe it's all too fast, too much. But I need you to know that I'm not leaving. I'm not running again. I've seen how wonderful you are, and I'm going to prove to you that I'm not some jackass." He pressed a kiss to her forehead. "Because you are special and wonderful, and I'm sorry I ever made you doubt that."

What could she possibly say to that?

*How* could she possibly respond to something so wonderful?

*How* could she possibly not panic about something so terrifying?

Because his words were . . .

Everything. Too much. Frightening. Terrifying. *Everything.*

"I know it's a lot to spring on you, a lot for you to believe when I just left you without a word. But . . ." His warm breath skated over her skin. His voice was soft, gentle. "Let me take care of you."

"I—"

"Please, just for tonight. Let me stay. Let me help you. Let me prove to you that I mean everything I said."

Heidi should have told him to go, for self-preservation, to keep her self-respect, to make certain she could keep her heart safe. But . . . she couldn't make herself form the words to tell him to leave.

Instead, she just gave in to the need in her heart, her soul.

"Okay," she whispered.

# ELEVEN

## Brad

ONE WORD that made everything inside him settle.

His heart had been thudding in his chest, filling him with terror, thinking again about all the ways he wasn't smooth and charming. God, how was it possible to have bungled this more, to have not explained properly, making her think he'd say all those things but then just toss her aside . . .

Add in scaring her into falling down a fucking hill and making her injure herself and—

She shivered.

Fucking hell.

Still fucking up.

He grabbed a towel from the rack just outside the curtain, turned off the stream of water, and wrapped it around her. Snagging one for himself so he didn't drip on her floor, he wrapped it around his hips then carefully lifted her out of the shower.

"Why didn't you take off my underwear?" she whispered into his chest.

"I didn't want you to think I was trying to get you naked."

She snorted. "You mean, you're *not* trying to get me naked?"

Something inside him relaxed, and he shifted so he could meet her eyes. "I'm *always* trying to get you naked."

A quirk of that luscious mouth as he set her on the counter.

"I'll grab you some pajamas."

"I'm guessing they're somewhere in the middle of my floor, considering I was doing just that when you went all caveman on me."

He lifted a brow but couldn't deny she was right. Instead, he just went into the bedroom, spied the pajamas, along with some underwear that reminded him of the ass-hugging pair she was wearing, made even huggier—was that a word? Probably not—by the water. Regardless, they were plastered to her honey gold skin in a way that had made his cock stand at rigid attention.

Not unusual, since this woman seemed to do that to him just by breathing.

Add in tight fabric and see-through lace, and he was a goner.

She'd slipped off her bra by the time he returned, had spread it on the towel next to her.

"Here," he said, handing her the pajamas and looking away.

Not leaving though, and also not stopping himself from glancing at her out of the corner of his eye, from seeing the pink tip of her nipple, the swaying globe of her breast.

Pervert?

Yup.

But he had to make sure she didn't fall.

That was the only reason he stayed. Simply for safety purposes.

When she went to slip off the counter, after she'd tugged the pajama top over her head, he stepped forward, lifted her down.

Her lips parted, a hot, damp exhale coating his skin.

But she didn't push him away, not even when he reached for

the waistband of her underwear and worked the wet material down her thighs, bending further to bring it past her knees, lifting one foot then the other to slip it off.

She released another shaking exhale, but it wasn't like his breathing wasn't steady either.

Still, he backed up a pace, handing her the dry underwear and pajama bottoms, and turning away.

Movement behind him, the soft sound of fabric sliding over naked skin. Then a warm palm on his back. "I have some clothes that should fit you in my closet."

"I'm fine," he told her.

"How are those wet boxer briefs feeling about now?"

Not great.

They weren't feeling great, but she had bigger things to worry about other than his chafing issues.

"Fine."

"Brad," she warned.

"How's your ankle?" He moved to lift her up again, readying to carry her to the bed.

"Fine," she said, brushing past him.

Well, *limping* past him.

"Heidi." It was his turn to warn.

"Not so fun, is it?" she muttered, making her way through a door that was attached to the bathroom.

He did some muttering of his own. "No, it isn't." Following her, he saw it was walk-in-sized, and one look around the space told him that Heidi had a *lot* of clothes—though they seemed to only come in the T-shirts and jeans variety.

"You have an extensive collection of graphic tees," he pointed out as she hobbled toward the far side and stood on tiptoe.

She turned one on a hanger, showing him that it had the words *This T-shirt is the color of my soul.* It was black and had him fighting back a smile. "That's because they express me better than *I* can express me." A shrug. "Plus, I don't have to wear adult clothes very often. I love my tees. *And* my pajamas. Half my dresser is filled with them, and I can honestly say that I've probably spent more on them than anything else in my wardrobe, combined."

He ran a finger over the silk sleeve of her pajama top. It was soft and cut high to expose a large portion of her arm. "I like them."

She glared over her shoulder, wavering to the side so much that he had to catch her shoulder to steady her. "Because you've seen the underwear I have on beneath them?"

"That *is* a plus," he said, finally realizing what she was reaching for, and nudging her to the side so he could snag the large plastic tub before she forgot she was hurt and started scrambling up the shelves.

"Where do you want this?" he asked.

"Open it up, help yourself to the clothes inside." A shrug. "My exes won't care. I promise."

Like it had burned him, he dropped the box on the floor.

Heidi laughed. "I'm kidding," she said, opening the lid. "My dad left these behind when he stayed over a while back. They're clean and free from any ex cooties." She tugged out a pair of sweats, a hoodie, and a T-shirt, handing them over. "No underwear, I'm afraid, but I'm guessing you don't want to wear another man's boxer briefs."

"No."

She snorted. "You look like you swallowed a lemon."

"Maybe just a lime," he muttered, freezing when she snagged the shirt from his hands and tugged it over his head.

A pat to his chest, her lips curved into a smirk, but there were deep lines etched into the space around her mouth.

"You should lie down," he said.

For once, she didn't argue, just nodded. "I think you're right. I'm actually starting to feel a bit dizzy."

He dropped the clothes, snagged her arm when she wavered. "Did you hit your head when you fell?" He'd seen the cut on her cheek, knew it had looked worse than it was. After he'd cleaned it, he'd realized it was just a scratch. He could also see that her ankle was bothering her, and maybe her hip. But he didn't think she'd hit her head. Still, she'd fallen so fast he couldn't be sure.

"No," she said. "I think it's just the adrenaline coming down." She pulled her arm free. "Well, that and the fact that I didn't eat lunch."

God save him from this woman.

He bit back a snarl, wanting to yell at her for not taking care of herself. Yes, he knew her particular predicament was his fault. But that didn't give her an excuse to not fuel her body. First the cell phone, now skipping lunch.

A pat to his jaw. "More lemon-swallowing." She turned and made her way carefully out of the closet, shuffling across the bedroom to her bed. "Stop hovering," she muttered. "I can make it five feet to the bed. If you really want to make yourself useful, why don't you go get me a bag of ice?"

That was an excellent point.

But he still made sure she'd made it into bed.

A fact that didn't escape her notice. Probably because he was currently tucking the covers up and over her.

"I didn't take you for one of these men."

He'd just straightened, and her words made him frown. "What do you mean?"

"Manly. Caveman. Protective."

Some of the fear that had gripped him since seeing her fall, since he'd thought she was going to kick him out because he kept flubbing things with her, faded. Enough for him to say, "I don't know whether to be insulted or complimented. You think I'm manly?" He fluttered his lashes. "Oh, thank you."

She snorted. "Ice, please, Mr. Caveman."

"For the record," he said, heading for the kitchen. "I'm always protective." A beat. "Especially, when it comes to a woman who matters."

"Brad—"

But he was just going to let that statement hover in the air.

He took the opportunity to escape into the hall.

# TWELVE

Heidi

SHE JUST STARED at Brad's retreating back and tried to figure out what in the fuck she was doing.

Getting naked in front of him—or naked in intervals, she supposed.

Showering clothed with him—or more like showering *semi-*clothed with him.

Talking with him—as though it were no big deal to have this man in her bedroom, casually discussing her pajama and T-shirt collection.

It *was* a big deal, and he'd said . . .

A lot.

Too much, probably, but she was good at isolating parts of her brain, at pushing things down. Because part of her *couldn't* believe it—not because she didn't think it was possible for a man to really like her, to want to look after her, and be with her.

But because she didn't believe *this* man could feel that for her.

And back into circles she went.

She liked Brad, sincerely enjoyed spending time with him. She just . . . didn't trust him.

"You're asking too much, Heid," she murmured. "You *want* too much."

Now *that* was her mother talking, always telling Heidi to lower her expectations. *"No one wants to listen to a female scientist."* That was when she'd announced she wanted to be a physicist, like her dad, in kindergarten. *"Girls aren't good at math. You should take Home Economics, learn some real skills."* That had been in high school, when she'd been testing into calculus and applying to colleges. *"You should stop going to school before no man ever wants to marry you."* That had been just before she'd received her PhD. *"You work too much. You'll never have a family if you keep going like this. Men want their women to be home."*

That had been last week.

Good times.

The worst part of it was that she did want to have a family of her own. She wanted to get married and have babies, to bemoan dirty diapers, to get a pet—though definitely not one as unruly as the Fuzz—and to have her washing machine break down and have to go to Lowe's to buy a new one. She wanted to have all of those things.

She just also wanted to have her career.

Why was that so difficult?

These were modern times, with modern women and men. Jason Momoa could wear a pink scrunchie, for God's sake. Harry Styles could pose on the cover of a magazine in a skirt. Transgender and gay rights were expanding—she wasn't so naïve as to consider those rights were already equal to hers as a white, cis person, but strides were being made. People of all genders and color and sexual orientations were living their lives and standing up for equality.

So, why couldn't she just work at a job she loved *and* have a family she loved?

Why did her mom seem to think she had to sacrifice one for the other?

She didn't mind having a man in her life, one who gave her input on her choices, so long as her partner was open to her having the same input on his. She certainly didn't mind Brad's strength, the way he'd swooped down the hill, how he'd clearly been worried for her, but he had to also not mind her swooping in to save the day just as often.

If she cooked, he could do the dishes.

If she worked late, he should figure out dinner.

If she wanted to go somewhere, she didn't need his permission, though she had no problem offering a check-in.

Because wasn't that what partners in life and love were supposed to do?

Support one another. Be there for each other. Love despite flaws and shoulder the burdens of his life on occasion because she knew that he'd shoulder them for her just as often.

*That* was the kind of man she wanted.

But maybe he didn't exist.

Maybe it was a fantasy. Maybe *that* was why she was single. *Maybe* that was why she would never have a family, like her mother threatened.

She wanted a unicorn.

And, as much as she hated to admit, unicorns did not fucking exist. Well, they definitely didn't exist outside of her glorious unicorn of a job. She supposed that *was* existing, at least in one form, so maybe she should qualify her thought. Men as unicorns didn't exist.

Brad walked back in, the T-shirt she'd given him fitting snugly on a chest she'd been nose-close to not long before, one she'd spent plenty of time kissing months before. He was definitely yummy, but again . . . she didn't trust him.

Didn't trust that he could be what she wanted.

It would be easy, so fucking easy to just invite him to join her in bed and to have her merry way with him—when she wasn't feeling lightheaded or like her groin was a rubber band that had been stretched too far. But wouldn't that discount all of those things she wanted, push aside that unicorn she was searching to find, even if she could somehow compartmentalize that this was a fling and nothing more, and that she could never expect to find a note or receive a goodbye.

Except . . . he'd left a note.

Except . . . she'd told him how his disappearing had made her feel, and last night, when she'd passed out on him during the movie, he'd—sort of sweetly, she might add—tucked her into bed, fully clothed, and then had left her a note.

A man who changed.

Perhaps she'd found her unicorn, after all.

He handed her the ice pack then started to sit on the bed, before hesitating and straightening. "Let me go finish changing first," he said and turned, disappearing into the closet.

She couldn't deny that she watched his yummy ass bounce as he made his way.

*Perv.*

Yes, she supposed she was.

Well, she'd just chalk it up as another of her unenviable qualities—career-driven, bossy, outspoken, workaholic, and a total perv.

And that was just the short list.

A minute later, Brad reappeared, his arms full of clothes and towels. "I saw your washer's in the hall," he said. "I'll just start a load."

Heidi's mouth dropped open.

But he was already gone, and when he stuck his head in a little later, telling her to make herself comfortable and he was going to call for pizza, her mouth fell open a second time.

Make herself comfortable?

With him puttering his way around her place doing laundry?

And apparently also making a salad as an appetizer, which he filled with corn and shredded chicken and beans, all of which she didn't remember being in her kitchen, but must have been, otherwise the man had mysterious pantry stocking abilities—either that or Instacart, she realized after she'd dopily stared for several minutes at the salad that was more filling than most meals she ate on a regular basis.

He'd set the TV remote on the nightstand, retrieved the book she'd left propped open on her coffee table—much to her chagrin, since she never seemed to be able to organize her books all that well.

She was always pulling down an old favorite and rereading part of it, jumping to her favorite scenes before forgetting to put it back.

Once a week, she forced herself to do a focused walk-through of her place, gathering those half-read books and stashing them back on the bookcase—in alphabetical order by genre, of course.

But that wasn't important.

Okay, it *was* important, just not important to this exact moment, because what was truly important right then was the fact that Brad was being . . . well, The Unicorn.

Without a word, without being asked.

He was just being . . . Brad.

And by the time he brought a plate of pizza to her, her resolution to stay far away from him was steadily being chipped away. Hell, the truth was that had been gone the evening of the wedding. What she felt chipping away in this moment was her resolve to keep the man firmly in the friend zone. Because it was as though he'd picked the thoughts out of her brain and had manifested himself into that Unicorn.

Pretty man.

Nice man.

Helpful man.

*Unicorn.*

Heidi was being sucked down in the whirlpool, that resolve dripping to the wayside, her need for him taking its place, and growing, and even worse—what would be even more devastating to her heart, to all of those carefully held dreams she worried about ever coming true—she worried she was falling for him all over again.

"God," she hissed, tossing the remote on the bed next to her with a groan.

She needed to stop living in her head.

She needed to stop circling this dead horse.

Did she want to have a fling with Brad, even knowing that despite the pretty words, it would inevitably end?

Yes.

She . . . just didn't want the broken heart.

This was like one of the calculations she was so good at, only except for detecting the space between electrons or attempting to figure out the top-secret shit (the speed of those electrons and how they moved, so it might be implemented for communication across the globe), this one was more . . . cost-benefit for her heart.

And if one night had dinged her confidence, had her thinking about this man for months, so on edge now, when they were hardly friends, what would a relationship do? What would happen when she grew attached and then he said goodbye?

But what if he didn't?

She groaned again, sitting up and shoving her mouth full of the pizza he'd brought her.

Self-medicating with food.

Because she already knew what her answer was going to be —even despite all the whirling thoughts in her head.

Because whatever anyone might say about Heidi's faults . . .

She wasn't a coward.

# THIRTEEN

Brad

SOMETHING HAD SHIFTED.

He didn't understand exactly what it was, except that it was as though someone had pricked the barrier holding the atmosphere of the room, the air that always seemed to ripple with awareness, with a pin, and the tension was slowly leaking out, a balloon deflating molecule by molecule.

He'd folded Heidi's now clean and dry clothes.

He'd changed back into his original, also clean and dry, had put the temporaries back in her bin, that bin back on the shelf. He'd fed her—once with salad because he was too freaking worried about her having not eaten all day to wait an hour for the second, which was the pizza he'd ordered, laden with meat and veggies to make up for that lack of lunch.

She'd gobbled down three pieces, moaning about how delicious it was, before later groaning and patting her stomach, saying that she'd need to invest in larger pajamas.

Now, he was sitting in a chair next to the bed, she'd turned on some reality TV show, and they were coexisting peacefully.

That tension continued to ebb away, along with his guilt, and he was starting to worry less, to actually enjoy himself.

Then she spoke.

And his heart seized.

"Brad."

She was going to kick him out. Well, fuck *that*. He wasn't going to leave her. He wasn't going to let her go without a fight. He needed to take a page out of his so-called manly book and dig in his heels.

"Brad?" she repeated.

He kept his eyes glued to the screen. "Yeah?"

"Come into bed with me."

Suddenly, the TV was nowhere in the periphery, his gaze flying to hers, locking onto hers. "What?"

She patted the pillow next to her. "That chair's not comfortable, and you're going to get a crick in your neck. Come relax with me."

"Crick—" He shook himself. "Neck—"

Pushing her elbows up beneath her, she reached out and snagged his hand. "Brad. Honey," she murmured. "I'm inviting you into bed with me."

But he hadn't won her over yet. He hadn't shown her that she could trust him.

Hadn't—

*Dumb shit.* He needed to get his ass in gear.

Shoving out of the seat, he crawled in beneath the blankets next to her, initially leaving a couple of feet between them, then deciding, what the hell, and sliding closer, slipping his arm beneath her, shifting his body so they were pressed together, shoulders to thigh.

"How's your ankle?"

She pointed and flexed it a few times beneath the covers. "Better. The ice helped."

He made a face.

"I saw that."

"How could you see that?" he asked, smoothing a hand up and down her spine. "Your face is in my chest."

"Fine. I *sensed* it."

"Sensed what?" He was playing dumb.

And he was rewarded for his acting skills when she tilted her head back so she could glare up at him. "Sensed *that*," she grumbled, waving a hand in the direction of his face. "More lemon-swallowing."

"I hate that you got hurt because of me."

She sighed. "Yes, you startled me." She pushed up farther. "But no, you're not responsible for my clumsiness. Nope. That all comes from me. Want to ask the room at large who's the girl who once managed to stab her hand and toe with the same knife? Or the one who burned herself because she was in too much of a hurry trying to make breakfast once and managed to catch both her hair and the hem of her T-shirt on fire at the stove. Oh, and that doesn't include the time I broke my wrist skiing, the concussion I received from walking into the open door of a locker, or the torn ACL when I tripped walking up the stairs."

He paused, hand stilling on her back. "*Up* the stairs?"

A grin. "Yup. You heard that right. I tripped going up the stairs, right in front of school my sophomore year." She rolled her eyes. "I actually tore it so badly that I had to have surgery. Don't laugh!" she accused when he attempted to bite back a smile.

Fingers brushing over her cheek, her jaw. God, her skin was like silk. But he also loved the look in her eyes, the teasing expression on her face. "I still can't believe you tripped up the stairs."

"I told you *not* to laugh."

"I'm not." But he was chuckling now, his chest vibrating with the sound, even as he kept taking this opportunity to touch her.

He might not be smooth, but he wasn't dumb.

He'd ended up in bed with the woman he wanted, and he wasn't going to squander this opportunity.

Now, to get her as addicted to his presence as he was to hers. Cue evil laughter, plotting-to-take-over-the-world hand rubbing.

"Like I said," she muttered. "I'm klutzy, and it has nothing to do with you."

"Well, next time, I'll make sure to not frighten you near inclines." Or declines either, he supposed.

"Cora always says I'm likely to kill myself just walking down the street to 7-Eleven to get a slushie."

"Remind me to never let you out of my sight," he said, half-joking.

Only half, because he was half-serious, too. Broken bones and torn ligaments and twisted ankles. Burns and stab wounds. God, he shuddered to think of what might go wrong in that top secret lab of hers.

She could blow up herself and the world right with her.

"The only place I'm somehow not clumsy—" A smile before she relaxed back down on his chest. "No, it's two places. One at work—and mostly because I have computers to do the dirty work, assistants to handle any of the finicky work, and anything I have to do is usually stationary, so there is significantly less chance of my klutz skills to factor in."

He smoothed a hand down her hair. "And the other?"

Her chest rose and fell on a long exhale. "The other place is . . . ice skating."

"Ice skating?" he asked incredulously.

"Yup." A laugh. "And I know exactly what you're thinking."

Nope. She couldn't. Because he was wondering how many

stab wounds he might end up with if blades were strapped to her feet. He assumed it would be a great many.

"You're thinking that with my amazing clumsy skills, that someone is going to end up bleeding out on the ice."

He bit the inside of his cheek to keep from laughing out loud.

"See?"

"See what?" he asked.

"See, that I am—" A yawn. "Exceptionally smart. Even if I do watch"—another yawn—"horrible TV as you accused."

"Well, I don't understand the appeal of watching people who don't even like each other stumble their way to the altar."

She gasped, sitting up and the fatigue slipping out of her pretty hazel eyes. "They like each other. They love each other. They've moved across the planet to see if they're compatible—"

"Or for a green card."

Heidi paused, considered that. "Yes," she agreed. "I do think that sometimes that's the case."

"I'll add very smart to your list of positive attributes, right along with talented at work, ice skater extraordinaire, and—*oh, how did you learn how to skate? Didn't you tell me once that you grew up in California?"

A smile. "All of last night," she said. "I did tell you that."

"So, Cali girl somehow learns to do a popular low-temperature activity?"

She shuddered, settled back down on his chest. "Okay, first rule for my new Californian. Don't call it Cali."

"No Cali." He nodded. "Got it."

"The second rule—or I guess less rule and more . . . general knowledge that you can put to good use is that hockey is big in California. It is especially big in Northern California, and because of that, there are plenty of opportunities for skating in the area."

"Noted," he said. "So, does this mean you'll go ice skating with me?"

"Are you asking me on a date?"

"Are you going to say yes?"

"Isn't ice skating a little pedantic of a date for you?"

He smiled. "I don't know." A shrug. "Depends."

"Depends on what?"

"On whether or not you say yes."

She laughed, arms tightening around him. "I'd say yes."

Joy bubbled in him. "Okay then, will you go ice skating with me, Heidi Greene?"

"No."

His jaw dropped open.

"But I *will* go on a date with you." A beat. "Even if it's ice skating."

He blinked, trying to keep up with the circles this woman was spinning around him and understanding that he probably never would be able to. Then he shrugged, began tracing light circles on her back again, and decided he didn't care.

Not when it meant that he'd just scored a date with this woman.

# FOURTEEN

Heidi

HE DIDN'T TAKE her ice skating.

But he did take her to prison.

To Alcatraz, that was.

"It's funny," she said as they leaned against the railing of the ferry, wind blowing through their hair, The Rock, coming into view in the distance.

"What's funny?" he asked.

"I grew up here, and I've never done any of the touristy things. No Alcatraz, no cable cars or Lombard Street. Hell, I've only ever done Ghirardelli Square and Pier 39 when relatives visited and wanted to hit the tourist traps."

"Well, there are far more exciting things to see in California besides the stuff that makes it on the postcards."

"That's true." She turned to look at him. "So, why bring me here?"

"You only agreed to one date," he said, eyes twinkling. "This is my backup plan in case you don't agree to a second."

She laughed. "Backup plan because you'll lock me up until I agree to it?"

"Precisely," he said. "Either that, or I hope that you'll be so bored with the history that you'll fall asleep, and then I can have my way with you."

"So romantic," she muttered dryly.

A swathe of pink exploded on his cheeks. "I—shit—I didn't mean it that way. I wouldn't take advantage of you—"

She touched his hand. "I know you wouldn't."

"I just meant in the sense of an evil genius taking over the world, not that I would do something you didn't want." He winced. "Shit. I sound like an asshole."

She rested her palm on his chest. "It was a joke," she assured him. "I got it. So, maybe it's not the best one I've heard"—a smile—"but I'm glad you at least understand consent, and how something like that might not land properly. You're a very evolved man," she added lightly.

He rolled his eyes.

But she was serious.

He was thoughtful and compassionate . . . and protective, while also doing laundry. Capable, a little bossy without minding when she pushed back . . . and he also made coffee.

Maybe he truly *was* the Unicorn.

She felt herself slide a little deeper down the rabbit hole.

Especially when she glanced up into those hazel eyes to see them edged with concern. "Plus," she said. "I *am* interested in the history. I heard a lot about Alcatraz growing up, so I'm excited to expand my knowledge of all things tourist trap."

He relaxed, capturing a strand of her hair that had escaped her ponytail in the gusty winds and tucking it behind her ear. "Should we walk across the Golden Gate next?"

"Yeah, no," she said, shuddering. "That's a step too far for me in my newly-donned tourist hat." Snorting and shaking her head, she watched the ferry slice through the surf, the bay water blue tinged with brown and breaking into whitecaps as it bounced against the hull. It was chilly, fall turning into winter, and yet with Brad next to her, standing close enough that his entire body was surrounding hers and blocking the wind, she was perfectly comfortable.

Silence lapsed between them as they both took in their course across the Bay, and though it was beautiful, the fog curling in ribbons across the sky, Heidi couldn't help but reflect on the week. It had been precisely fourteen days since she, Brad, and Fuzzy McFeatherston had participated in their cake disaster, but it felt like a lifetime ago.

They'd had nine nights together.

Nine nights that ranked up there with the best ones of her life, even though they'd hardly done anything—just eaten together, watched TV, cuddled on the couch . . . and in her bed.

Yes, that fact terrified her.

But . . . she was firmly addicted and had just decided to accept her fate.

She'd ride this ride to the end, and hopefully, knowing that there would be an end meant that her heart wouldn't hurt so much when Brad decided to flit off.

Or—her pulse thrummed with possibility—maybe he'd stay and—

*Enough.*

So, yes, these last two weeks had been wonderful, filled with easy conversation and warm arms. The evening of her creek shenanigans he'd stayed late, watching bad reality TV and then the various segments from all the late-night shows posted on YouTube that had struck her fancy before finally slipping out around midnight. He'd pressed a kiss to her forehead, leaving her drowsy and snuggly tucked under the covers. And when she'd woken up the following morning, it was to find that he'd prepped her coffee pot to automatically brew and had left a muffin under some plastic wrap on a plate on the counter.

Then that night, he'd coaxed her from work to Molly's for dinner.

Okay, truthfully, it hadn't taken much coaxing . . . because Molly's.

And while dinner wasn't quite as good as breakfast—because they didn't have the normal amount of freshly made baked goods—it was *almost* as good. They'd scarfed down hot sandwiches made on freshly made bread, had slurped up steaming soup laden with veggies and plenty of potatoes, and she'd washed down the huge portion with the best pomegranate iced tea she had ever tasted.

And then they'd gone back to her place to watch more bad reality TV—though this time it was from her couch and not her bed—and he'd left around midnight again.

The following evening, he'd called to say he'd gotten stuck in traffic returning from a beach in Santa Cruz, so they hadn't hung out, hadn't cuddled on the couch. And . . . she'd missed it.

Which had made her stomach squeeze, her pulse flutter.

Because she'd known then that she was already hooked on Brad.

Hooked on the dangerous, dangerous man.

But he hadn't seemed to notice her disquiet—or maybe he *had*, she realized, remembering the conversation and how he'd drawn her back in with a funny anecdote, how he'd continued to talk with her until she'd relaxed again.

*Then* he'd finagled an invite to her condo the next night.

He still hadn't stayed over, and she hadn't asked him to, even though she'd wanted to.

He'd just kissed her on the forehead again then slipped out the front door.

And wash, rinse, and repeat.

He'd coaxed her to Molly's for breakfast one day before work—saying he just *had* to try the freshly baked pastries. Another evening they'd walked hand-in-hand on the trails behind her house. Two nights ago, he'd shown up with a big bag of takeout without a word, not long after she'd mentioned that work that day had been exhausting. And on the couple of days he was off doing Brad things and not cuddled up with her on her couch, he'd called just to chat, and they'd ended up talking for hours.

More light, fun times. More warm conversations. More forehead kisses.

And now it was Saturday, and she was here with him. On a date.

And somehow, she knew there would be no more forehead kissing.

Or maybe, more accurately, it would be replaced with a *different* kind of kissing. Her body liked that thought. Her heart was hopeful. Her brain . . . well, it had already decided it was going to take a back seat to the rest of her.

"Wow," he murmured.

Heidi blinked, reorienting herself as she realized they'd arrived at the dock on the edge of the island located in the middle of the Bay, the decommissioned prison sitting atop it. There were more buildings than she'd expected, and it was also taller, with sharp cliffs leading almost straight down to the bay.

"You better not fall down this one," Brad murmured into her ear.

She laughed, startled. "You're joking about it now?"

"I've witnessed several more of your so-called clumsy skills," he said, his hot breath still on her skin and making her shiver.

"Do you remember the incident just last night when you somehow managed to get your hair stuck on the knob of the cabinet?"

She remembered all right.

She also remembered the gentle fingers untangling the strands, the way her body had reacted so intensely to his proximity.

"Rude," she muttered, even though she was definitely affected by his proximity even now. A woman had to have *some* pride, and if she couldn't muster at least a modicum of sarcasm, where would she be?

"The truth," he said. "And my point is that I think I can afford a small joke."

She wrinkled her nose. "At least this one is better than your prison joke."

He hissed out a breath. "Ouch, that's cold," he said, stepping back and taking her hand. "You're right, but damn, that's cold."

Giggling, she tugged him toward the stairs that would take them to the bottom level of the ferry, where they could disembark. "Come on, I need to get my audio tour and visit the gift shop."

"And here I'd prepared myself to play tour guide," he said dryly as they hit the bottom step. "I even have one of those little flowers so you can easily find me in the crowd."

"Do you really?"

His expression went serious, and he reached into his back pocket.

Her mouth dropped open.

But then he grinned, holding up his empty hand. "Seriously, though, I did do some research before coming. Redoing the visitor's center's website is next on my client list."

"Isn't it run by the government?"

"I have a contract with the government," he said and leaned close. "And now that I've told you that, I have to kill you."

She swatted him. "Stop joking around," she told him. "Because seriously, that's awesome. How long have you had the contract?"

"For a few years. The actual National Parks Service site is run and managed by the government—I would never have the capacity to set up something so vast. But a lot of the visitor's centers and tourist attractions are run by an outside company." He shrugged. "I did that company's main site maybe five years back, and then a higher up in the tech department asked me to do a spread for Crater Lake. Now, I've been slowly working my way through a lot of the national parks' visitor interfaces. They do the actual functionality and building. I just advise on design and useability." He continued to hold her hand as they walked down the gangway. "Next week is Alcatraz, and since it's here, I figured now would be as good a time as any to see The Rock."

"Wow. That's really impressive."

Another shrug. "Not really, and certainly there wasn't any skill involved," he said, "I'm just lucky that this fell into my lap and I could make a career out of it."

"They wouldn't keep you on if you weren't good."

He glanced down at her, eyes dancing. "Don't you know anything about our government? It's a giant pile of incompetence and overspend."

"Ah, *so* optimistic," she teased.

"Realistic is more like it."

"Okay then," she declared. "I will be the barometer of all things talented. You'll show me a portfolio of your work, and I shall decree whether or not you're worthy."

He tugged a lock of her hair, blowing in the breeze. "Should I get you a crown, too?"

She fought back a smile. "Obviously." A beat. "And a scepter."

He mimed making a note. "I've got it on my mental checklist."

"More like your mental *bullshit* meter," she said.

A tap to his nose. "Ding. Ding. Ding."

She glanced up at him, totally losing her fight with the smile, seeing that he wore an answering one in return. "I also feel obligated to point out," she said, "that you've taken me on a date so you can work."

His mouth dropped open.

"Am I right?"

He shook his head, a band of pink appearing on his cheeks. "No, I— That's not what I was doing. I just thought that since you said you hadn't seen a lot of touristy things and I was getting ready to work on this that—"

"Work," she repeated in a sing-song voice.

His lips parted. Closed. Parted again. "Shit. I'm an asshole."

She went on tiptoe, let her mouth drift close to his ear, and felt a thrill weave through her when he shivered, at knowing that he was just as affected by her as she was by him. "But you're *my* asshole," she whispered.

He turned his head, eyes blazing with emotion as they met hers. Then his lips quirked. "Yes, I am."

Heart pounding at the undertones in the conversation, knowing that neither of them was sincere about the asshole part, Heidi forced her gaze away and concentrated on just breathing. They'd reached solid ground. The ferry-load of people were weaving their way up the path to enter the historic site, and they were all but alone under the partly cloudy day, the wind in their air, the faint scent of the Pacific Ocean just beyond the Golden Gate filling her nose.

It was a beautiful day with a beautiful man, and she was

having the time of her life just chatting and joking and walking with him.

If that wasn't the Unicorn, she didn't know what was.

And that was when Heidi lost her battle with self-control.

Rising up on tiptoe, she kissed him.

And not on his forehead, either.

# FIFTEEN

Brad

HE WAS STUNNED into stillness for a heartbeat.

Then he kissed her back.

He'd been thinking how beautiful she was with the sunlight dappling her skin, the wind ruffling her hair, the laughter dancing in her eyes. He'd been *thinking* how much he wanted to kiss her, how hard it was becoming to resist the urge.

And now she'd just tugged him to the side of the path, had pressed her soft, curvy body to his, and kissed him.

His lips parted automatically, his tongue sweeping forward to tangle with hers, tasting the faint hint of coffee and chocolate and banana on her tongue—the woman was obsessed with those muffins, and he was going to do his damndest to keep up with her demand for them. But it wasn't off-putting, even though he wasn't a big fan of either chocolate or banana. Instead . . . it was coming home. It was Heidi.

It was perfect.

So perfect, in fact, that he'd dipped his hands under her

shirt, fingertips brushing the silken skin of her abdomen on the appetizer to heading north when he felt a tap on his shoulder.

"You can't do that here," the female voice said.

He pulled back, blinked dazedly as he turned, trying to get his bearings. "I'm sorry, what?"

His vision cleared enough to remind him where he was, for him to see that it wasn't just a woman standing behind them, but a guard with an official badge and uniform and intense-looking duty belt.

The guard lifted an eyebrow. "I'd suggest you either start your tour, or you end it."

Heidi giggled—one pure burst of sound that had Brad fighting back a smile. "I'm sorry," he said. "We'll go get started."

The guard nodded. "Carry on—" Her eyes narrowed. "Well, not *carry on*"—she waved a hand—"but please, proceed with touring the facility."

Another tiny giggle that did nothing for his self-control, but he managed to stumble out another apology, to tug a chortling Heidi up the path and away from the guard, all without them getting thrown in the brig or finding themselves packed onto the next ferry back to the mainland.

"Your fault," he muttered.

"Yours." A beat. "You need to stop being so charming."

"I can't help it," he said. "It's a gift."

"One the entire world gets to benefit from?" she asked archly.

"Exactly." He stopped just past the turnstile after they'd paid for their tickets and glared down at her. "But as for the point at hand, I seem to remember *you* as the one doing the kissing."

She sidled closer. "I seem to remember *you* kissing me back."

Well, she had him there.

"Come on," he said, instead of conceding the point. They picked up their audio guide—Heidi had wisely opted out of his tour—then put on their headphones as they walked into the first room.

Cavernous. Cold. Gloomy.

He hated it instantly, and the audio of the tour wasn't much better, adding to the oppressiveness of the place, making him regret that he'd even thought to bring her here, especially on a date.

She slipped her headphones off, glancing around the room, eyes dimmed.

"Let's go," he said.

Her brows pulled together. "What? We just got here."

"I hate it," he muttered.

"Well, it certainly isn't sunshine and rainbows," she said, "but don't you have something for work you should be doing?"

Asked so innocently that he nearly missed the teasing in her eyes.

"I'm not going to live that down, am I?"

"I'll pretend to forget about it if you pretend to forget I lost that battle with the cabinet knob."

"Done."

"Pleasure doing business with you," she said, sticking her hand out so he could shake it. "And I'm fine with going. I don't like it here either." A shiver. "Though part of me thinks we should push through and learn what we can."

"I get that." He nodded. "But I don't think we'd be learning much."

"Probably not. And . . . I guess it reminds me too much of what is wrong with the world." She made a face. "I mean, we *should* know, because otherwise how are we going to help fix things? It's just . . ."

He brushed his fingers over her cheek. "Probably not the best place for a date."

"Yes." Her lips tipped up at the corner. "*That*."

"Then we'll go do something else."

She smiled up at him. "So, how do we get out of here?"

"Same way you do with all these tourist traps." He brushed a finger down her nose. "Through the gift shop."

Laughing, she leaned close, weaving her arm through his. "Then lead on, oh master of all things travel-related."

He snagged her audio device, carrying both as they made their way through the cells, the cafeteria, the workrooms, the isolation room, weaving their path through the other patrons, pausing to take in a few signs with historical information, but for the most part, making their way to the exit as quickly as possible.

Which, unerringly, meant they ended up in the gift shop.

"Of course," she said as they stepped into the bright room, filled with racks of T-shirts and magnets and shot glasses and postcards. One entire wall had candy. Another held books. Heidi stopped by a set of dish towels and held them up. "Just what I always wanted."

"Come on, Trouble," he said, tugging them from her hands and putting them down on the stack. "Let's see if we can catch this ferry before it leaves."

A mock pout. "You owe me more shopping time at a future date."

He towed her toward the door, down the path toward the dock. "I'll remind you of our earlier conversation, in which you expounded on all things that are terrible about shopping."

"Yes, shopping in general," she said. "But not about the only type of acceptable shopping."

"What's that?" he asked as they boarded the ferry.

"Books." She smiled. "And there happens to be some amazing bookstores in San Francisco."

"Well," he said with tacit agreement as they both climbed the stairs. "Since my date idea was a bust, I think it makes sense to try yours. Should we hit up some of those bookstores instead?"

Her lips parted, surprise flitting in her eyes. "You're serious?"

Thumb tracing that plump bottom lip, he couldn't resist pulling her close, the scent of her shampoo tangling with that of the sea air. He couldn't get over how she seemed to fit perfectly against him, as though her body had been made for his, as though *she* had been made for him. "I'm serious," he said, unable to bite back a smile.

Joy lit up her face, and she did a little happy dance, one that had the positive benefit of brushing all those luscious curves against his body and one that made him lose his battle with control.

He dipped his head and kissed her.

And this time, there wasn't any guard around to make them stop.

At least until they arrived back in the city proper.

And *then* they got kicked off the ferry.

But seeing Heidi with swollen lips, her hair doubly messed from his fingers and the wind, her cheeks pink, and her eyes warm, and he decided a permanent ban from that ferry line was totally worth being able to kiss her.

Bar none.

# SIXTEEN

Heidi

SHE KEPT GLANCING over at Brad, expecting to see boredom creep into his face, but every time she stopped browsing to check in, his expression wasn't annoyed or impatient.

Instead, he almost seemed to be studying her, watching and filing away each movement.

He'd disappeared when she'd become engrossed in the historical romance section then had reemerged some quantity of time later—she really wasn't good at keeping track of the movement of the Earth around the sun when there were books in front of her—his hands holding a few novels.

And then she'd expected the impatience to start and so had quickly shifted her bundle, trying to hurry in her selections, even though there . . . were . . . just . . . so . . . many . . . choices!

But instead of telling her to make a pick, he'd just snagged the books she'd tucked under one arm and told her to, "Explore."

She'd fallen in love—just a little bit—with that one word.

*Explore.*

God, the man was a menace.

Now, she was running her pointer finger over the spine of one more book—this one being one she already owned, only she had the UK version at home and was trying to decide if she liked the US version enough to have two copies.

She started to push it back into place.

No. Her bookshelves were already overflowing as it was. She couldn't justify the second copy, especially with the stack that Brad was already carrying for her.

"Okay," she said, turning to him. "Your torture is over. Hand me my stack so we can go check out."

Except, as the last word slipped off her tongue, her cell phone rang.

"Sorry," she told him, reaching into her purse. "That ringtone is the lab."

"Go ahead and answer it." He nodded toward the exit. "I'll buy these and meet you out there."

She took a step, stopped, her cell in her hand. "I'll pay you—"

"*Go,*" he urged as her phone rang again. "We'll figure it out later."

"Thanks," she said, hustling out onto the street and answering the call. Her weekend lab assistant, Maggie, was on the other end.

"We have a problem . . ." she began.

And that was the moment Heidi realized her day with Brad was over.

Because problem was an understatement. A mere problem would have meant that she might have been able to handle it over the phone, or at worst, email in written instructions to follow. A problem might have meant that she needed to check on the lab tomorrow, just to make sure all was fixed.

This . . . *this* was a disaster.

This had her immediately barking instructions. It also had Brad—who'd come out of the bookstore with two giant bags—take one look at her face and instantly begin directing her to his car.

"Tell me where to go," he said when they'd gotten in and she'd paused in her orders.

She rattled off the address.

Ten seconds to put it into his cell, a quick lift in her direction so she could confirm the location was correct, and then a minute later they were on the road, winding through city streets jammed with pedestrians and Saturday traffic and eventually making their way to the freeway and hightailing it south.

"No," she exclaimed. "Don't shut it down." They'd lose everything. She spared a look at Brad's cell, perched in a cradle connected to the air vent. "We'll be there in ten minutes. Just keep the computers up and running, I'll adjust the machinery when we get there." Maggie said a few more things—mostly listing what she'd do to keep the computers working, but Heidi didn't hang up or get short. She knew that Maggie was panicked, especially since she hadn't been able to reach Stef, who was on call for the lab this weekend for just this type of issue.

Maggie was a new grad. She was smart as a whip and funny, but she was also a bit anxious and a definite perfectionist.

This had thrown her for an absolute loop.

Not to mention, if she hadn't caught the miscalibration, the entire experiment would have been ruined—six months of research would have amounted to absolutely nothing.

"Deep breaths," she said when Maggie had paused for air. "Everything will be fine."

She hoped, but that was beside the point.

"I-I hope so, Heidi."

"It was a good catch," she told her, "and we'll figure out the rest. Now, I'm going to hang up and call Stef again."

"O-okay."

A moment later she was dialing her lead assistant, the call ringing and ringing and ringing until—

"Hello?"

"Stef," she said. "It's Heidi. Why the hell haven't you picked up your phone? The computer's malfunctioned, and the readings are writing over one another, and—"

"I'm in the hospital."

*"What?"*

"Fred"—her ninety-pound golden retriever—"pulled me over this morning. I didn't think I'd done more than twist my ankle and got a few bruises, but then my foot swelled up like a balloon, and I couldn't walk on it." She released a shaking breath. "I think I'm going to need to have surgery."

"Shit," Heidi whispered.

"I know."

"I'll get the lab sorted and come straight over."

Stef inhaled sharply, her normal no-nonsense tone returning. "Absolutely not, this is supposed to be your weekend off. Damage control and then call in Matteo. He can cover the lab for the rest of the time."

Since she *had* planned on calling Matteo to take over, she didn't argue with Stef, just asked her a few questions about her injury and what hospital she was at. Because she sure as hell wasn't going to allow her assistant to go through that alone. Stef was good people, and she didn't have anyone in the area since she'd broken up with her boyfriend and he'd taken their friends.

Assholes.

Somewhere in the swirling in the back of her head, she made a mental note to make sure she, Cora, Kelsey, and Kate all brought the full-frontal attack into folding Stef into their friend group.

She needed some peeps—and ones that wouldn't disappear just because a boyfriend was a total twat-waffle.

"What room are you in?"

"Five-oh-four," Stef said. "And here I live until at least tomorrow. They don't think the surgeon will be able to see me until then."

"Oh no," Heidi murmured as she jotted the hospital name and the room number on a scrap of paper from her purse. Last thing she needed to do was forget one or the other with everything else going on. "Seriously?"

"Seriously. But don't worry, I'm comfortable and have plenty of bad cable TV to keep me company."

"What about a phone charger? Or a change of clothes? Or snacks? Or a book?" she asked, mind jumping between her friend being in the hospital and the lab.

"It's one night," Stef said. "Trust me, I've roughed it in worse places."

"Hang in there," she said as they approached the gate for the lab.

"Keep me posted on the equipment."

Hell no, she wouldn't, or at least not any more than what was necessary so Stef wouldn't worry and jeopardize her recovery. "I'll call you as soon as I can," she promised then hung up, stashing her cell and pulling out her badge. "I'm afraid they won't let you in without the proper clearance," she told Brad. "You'll have to drop me out here, and I'll grab an Uber home."

"I can wait," he began.

She touched his cheek. "I have no idea how long I'll be."

"I don't mind."

"Well, I do," she murmured. "I won't be able to concentrate in there if you're out here just twiddling your thumbs. Go home.

I'll call tonight if it's not too late. Tomorrow, if it is." Dropping her hand, she pulled her purse onto her shoulder. "You can just park over there," she said, pointing to the row of visitor spots before the gate.

He pulled to a stop and looked at her. "You sure you don't want me to wait?" A small smile. "I've got plenty of books to keep me busy."

She nodded. "Thank you for offering. That's sweet. But I'm sure." Pausing with her hand on the handle of the door, she made a face and said, "But I *am* sorry my work ruined our date."

"Don't worry about it," he told her. "Now I've got plenty of ammunition to tease you back."

"I think we're equal, and that's it."

He laughed. "Maybe you're right."

Hand still resting on the pull, she hesitated. "I don't want to go."

"I know, baby," he murmured, pressing a quick kiss to her mouth that had her pulse skyrocketing and her lips tingling before he pulled back. "But your work is important. Our stuff will hold."

She released a trembling breath, her heart squeezing tight, a mental billboard flashing *Unicorn. Unicorn. Unicorn!* across her mind. "Thank you," she whispered.

A sexy smile. "Get out of here before I kiss that look off your face. You've got work to do."

Heart full, she nodded, pulled the lever, and got out. She walked quickly to the gate and showed her pass. When they opened it for her, she glanced back, saw that Brad was still waiting for her, and waved.

He waved back then gestured at her to hurry up.

Laughing, she turned her back on the gate, on the visitor's parking lot, on Brad, and hustled into the lab, thinking that she'd definitely found the Unicorn.

She just wasn't sure how long he'd stick around.

---

LATER THAT NIGHT, *many* hours later, after things in the lab had stabilized and she'd managed to save their six months of work, she stumbled into the parking lot, bleary-eyed and exhausted, Maggie staggering alongside her.

Luckily, she didn't have to wait for a pickup, as Maggie had offered to get her home, and so they made their way over to her assistant's tiny hybrid.

A few minutes later, they were on the freeway, heading for Heidi's place.

"Thanks again for driving me home," she said, staring out at the dark sky, at the bright flashes of white and red lights surrounding them.

"Thanks again for not firing me," Maggie said lightly.

"That calculation wasn't your fault, and you know it." Heidi shook her head. "I honestly cannot think of what happened. All the numbers and settings were correct when I left yesterday, and we were the only ones in there."

A beat. "Except, we weren't the only ones in there."

Heidi frowned. "What do you mean?"

"Well, when I came in this afternoon to run the checks, I saw the cleaning crew leaving." She glanced over then back at the road. "I didn't think anything of it at first, and then after I noticed the readings, I was in too much of a panic to make sure the experiment didn't fail that I'd forgotten."

"And now you remembered."

A nervous look toward Heidi. "Yeah. I'm sorry, I didn't remember sooner."

"I'm not irritated with you," she said, digging around her purse and grabbing her cell. There were all sorts of notifications on the screen, but nothing from Stef, who'd texted a few hours before saying they were taking her into surgery after all. "I'm just pissed that the protocol wasn't followed, especially considering everything that could have been jeopardized." She forced her tone to stay even. "In fact, I think you probably deserve a raise for managing to get all of those half-life calculations on the backup hard drive before the data was erased."

"I—well—"

Heidi patted her arm. "You did good," she said. "I promise I'd tell you otherwise."

"Not *so* good," she muttered. "Otherwise I wouldn't have had to call in the boss on her day off."

"Meh. Won't be the first, nor the last. Now," she added, changing the subject before Maggie could go too far down the rabbit hole of feeling sorry for herself and/or feeling guilty for needing to call in backup. "Tell me all about what it's like to be twenty-two and living in the city. What do all the cool kids do for fun?"

She laughed. "What makes you think I'm remotely a cool kid?"

"Because you're twenty-two," Heidi pointed out.

"Trust me," Maggie said dryly. "That's not nearly enough." But she did share a funny story about a bar called Bobby's she'd gone to with girlfriends the previous weekend, and how the front room was super fun with cool décor and fun music, but that the back room was filled with outdated tunes . . . and people.

"I just was looking for the bathroom, and I swear, it was like the middle-aged club had unleashed a party back there. There was dancing and drinking, and the noise was *intense.* I swear, they were having more fun than we were in that front room."

"How old were these middle-aged people?" she asked, well-familiar with Bobby's and definitely knowing that she and her friends were relegated to the back room.

Far away from the cool kids out front.

"God," Maggie said, turning into Heidi's complex. "They must have been like . . . thirty-five, some even forty."

Heidi choked on a laugh.

She was thirty-three, nearing thirty-four.

Apparently, that was almost middle-aged.

Heaven help her.

"Thanks again," she said when Maggie stopped in front of her condo. "I'm so glad I didn't have to wait for an Uber."

Maggie smiled, nodded. "Thanks for being so cool about the lab."

With a quick goodbye, she closed the door and headed up to the front door of her place. Oh, she'd been cool with Maggie—one, because it wasn't her assistant's fault, and two, because even if it *had* been, people made mistakes.

But the cleaning staff going into her lab wasn't a mistake.

Or it wasn't a mistake any longer.

She'd had to have a conversation with occupational health about not allowing the general cleaning company into the room three times already since she began at the company less than a year ago.

*This* would mark a fourth.

And the fourth broken promise, and one that had nearly jeopardized everything.

So no, she wouldn't be the cool boss. Not any longer. In fact, she and several people were going to have a very stern conversation, and then *if* that didn't work, she was installing a fucking dead bolt herself, with a lock and key only she and her team had copies of.

In fact, she was looking up said locks and keys, just to be

preemptively prepared, when her phone buzzed with a text from Stef.

> *Why the hell did you send tall, dark, and handsome to look after me? Just saying, if he was my man, I'd have him under lock and key.*

The mirroring of her own thoughts should have been funny. Except . . . *what?* Sending tall, dark, and who?

But before she could ask that, Stef sent a picture of Brad, a vase of flowers in his hand as he placed snacks on a rolling table.

> *He says you arranged everything. Surgery is over, obviously. Apparently, it was less complicated than they thought.*

Heidi blinked, her fingers starting to type out a reply. But her cell buzzed again before she got there.

> *Thank you. I know I said I was fine, but even though I didn't want to admit it, I was scared. Knowing that someone was out there in the waiting room, looking after me, even though you'd sent him, made me feel better.*

She'd typed out another reply, something that probably barely made sense, because her mind was spinning. But that was okay, because she still didn't get to send it.

Her cell vibrated one last time.

> *Tell me all about it in the morning. Visiting hours are over, and I'm going to zonk out.*

Heidi stared at her phone screen for several moments then shook her head. And . . . then her gaze alighted on something else, something she'd missed when she'd first stumbled her way inside.

Her books were on her bookshelf. On the proper bookshelf —that being her To Be Read shelf. In the proper order—that being separated by genre then alphabetized by author name.

All except the title she'd been waffling about purchasing. The pretty US cover was slotted right next to the UK one on her already read shelves.

The hospital.

Her condo.

The books.

Her friend.

Brad, the *Unicorn* known as Brad, had some explaining to do.

# SEVENTEEN

Brad

THE KNOCK at his door made him frown.

It was late, and even though his family was pushy, they would definitely call first, especially considering it was nearing midnight.

Someone must be confused, knocking at the wrong apartment.

Maybe a DoorDash had gone wrong.

Sighing when the knock came again, he set aside his book—the thriller he'd picked up earlier that day, and one that also had him wondering whether it was Russian mafia men or a terrifying serial killer on the other side of that wood—and made his way to the door.

He checked the peephole—because Russian mafia men and terrifying serial killers—but when he saw who was on the other side, his mouth dropped open, and he scrambled to release the dead bolt.

"Heidi!" he exclaimed the moment he'd wrenched open the door. "What are you—?"

She poked a finger into his chest. "You," she snapped then slipped by him, striding into his apartment, her shining brown hair fanning out behind her like a cape. "*You!*" she exclaimed, spinning around to face him while he locked up. Her hands were on her hips, her legs were clad in pajamas, and her eyes flashed.

"Me?" he asked when it appeared that was all she was going to say.

Her lips pressed flat. Her chin lifted. "Why?" she asked. "Why did you do it?"

His brows drew together. "The books?" He figured it was time to fess up. "I borrowed your spare key that night when you were hurt. It was there on your little organizer thing, and I didn't want you to be sleeping with an unlocked door, and I know it was probably an invasion of your privacy to keep it, but I've been staying late and didn't want you to have to worry about getting up." He shrugged helplessly. "I probably shouldn't have used it today, but I just figured you might like to read one of the books you bought—"

"*You* bought."

He paused. "What?"

"*You* bought the books," she said. "Not me."

"I . . ." He hesitated, not sure where she was going with this. Her fury seemed to have dimmed somewhat, but she was still standing there, looking fierce and ready to avenge crimes. "I told you, we could figure that out later."

"It's later." She took a step toward him.

"Okaaay." He glanced around. "I probably have the receipt around here somewhere."

She took another step, her expression so intense that he found himself wondering about serial killers again. "But this isn't about the books," she said, coming even closer, until her scent filled his nostrils, until the soft curves of her breasts came into contact with his chest.

Between her smell, her body, the way she kept coming closer, until her front was flush against his, and he wasn't operating on all cylinders. "It isn't?" he asked, confusion battling with desire now.

He pushed the latter down. He didn't want to fuck things up with this woman.

Even though every cell in his body was telling him to yank her close and kiss her senseless, to haul her behind the screen and have a repeat of the night a few months ago.

She shook her head. "No."

"What is it about then?"

A sexy smile curving lips begging to be kissed, but her eyes were serious and sitting heavy on his. "Stef."

Oh. Shit.

She reached up and cupped his jaw. "Why did you do it?"

He could do nothing but tell her the truth. "You were worried about her." A shrug. "I saw her room number and the hospital on the note you wrote. I figured I'd just poke my head in and make sure she didn't need anything."

"And you brought her flowers?"

Shit. Was that what this was about? Did she think that because he brought Stef flowers that he was trying to hit on another woman? That he didn't want Heidi? That couldn't be further from the truth.

"Baby—"

"And snacks."

"I—uh—she's important to you and—"

Heidi rose on tiptoe and kissed him.

Brad felt as though he'd been electrocuted, the sensation was so acute, so absolute. Heat seared into him, arrowing straight for his cock. He froze for one long moment, reveling in the feel of her against him, her lips tangling with his, before he remembered he could touch.

Wrapping his arms around her waist, he pulled her even closer until he couldn't be sure where he ended and she began. Curves filling his palms, a soft mouth on his, her tongue a sleek dart in his mouth. He gave into his earlier urge, sweeping her up into his arms, groaning when she straddled his hips, thighs clamping around his pelvis and rocking against the hard length of his erection.

And then he carried her behind the screen to his bed.

Heidi tugged her mouth from his when he laid her on the mattress, following her down, sprawling beside her, the haze of desire edging into his vision. "You brought her flowers, you wonderful man." She cupped his cheeks, holding him still when he went to kiss her again. "And her favorite snacks, apparently. How did you know?"

He shrugged. "I didn't. I just made an educated guess based on how much you've been raving about those chocolate-covered pretzels," he admitted. "And then I figured I couldn't go wrong with Molly's." A smile. "Someone really smart might have mentioned that to me once or twice."

Her lips tipped up. "As I said, you wonderful man."

"You're not mad?"

Now her eyes danced with humor. "Does it *seem* like I'm mad?"

"Actually, now that you mention it . . ."

She snorted. "Shut up and kiss me before I forget how wonderful you are."

That was an exceptionally easy order for him to follow.

He lowered his mouth to hers . . .

And sparks.

Her fingers dug into his shoulders, kneading the muscles there, pulling him closer until he was fully on top of her, feeling every glorious curve. He had an immediate sense of belonging, of coming home, of . . .

Heidi.

Her scent, spicy and floral, filling his nose. Her lips parting so he could sweep his tongue inside. Her legs falling open, bringing their hips in perfect alignment. Desire was a rapidly growing tempest, yanking him this way and that, reminding him of how good it had been between them, the memories of all the places she liked to be touched, of *how* she liked to be touched flooding forward.

He wanted to do everything at once, *needed* to stroke and lick, to tear off her clothes and plunge home, to—

His conscience dug its claws sharply into the sides of his brain and shook it fiercely.

Because it had been two weeks since he'd begun his campaign to win her over.

*Only* two weeks.

And if he really wanted to show her that he was going to stick around, he couldn't just fall into bed with her again. Well, they were *already* in bed, but he couldn't sleep with her until she knew—

A moan slipped past her lips, vibrating into his mouth, her tongue twining with his, those legs that had fallen open lifting to wrap tightly around his waist.

Naked.

He needed her naked.

His conscience gripped tighter, dug those claws in further, shook him even more intensely.

Wrenching his head back, he broke the kiss, though one look at Heidi's face nearly had his conscience's hooks dislodging. Grabbing on to the threads of his control, he rested his forehead on her shoulder, sweat prickling on his nape, breaths coming in rapid intervals.

But being this close to her fabulous set of breasts didn't help his cause either.

Because they were inches away and tempting him and—

He sat up, put the entire length of the mattress between them.

"What's wrong?" she asked.

Brad wasn't able to form words yet. His cock had a fucking heartbeat and was pressing against the zipper of his jeans with a persistent ache that had him very close to forgetting why he'd backed off in the first place.

Which was why his only answer was a shake of his head.

The bed dipped, the consequence of his non-answer being that she came closer. Normally, a perfectly acceptable reaction. Normally, something he would have loved. But right then, right in that moment with him trying to remember all the reasons he could not jump on top of her like a rabid beast and have his merry way with her? Right then, her coming closer wasn't ideal.

She pressed close to his side, and fuck, that was heaven and hell all at the same time. Curves and woman—no, *this* woman. Because Heidi was temptation personified.

But she needed to know that he wasn't back in her life looking for a fantastic night. She had to understand what she meant to him, even if he'd only just discerned the meaning himself. He wanted this woman to comprehend the change she'd jumpstarted, the things she'd made him realize about himself, and she . . .

Fuck, he needed this woman to understand that he loved her.

That he'd fallen that first night and had run because she'd pushed beyond the barriers surrounding his heart, even if he hadn't quite understood the panicked reaction until two weeks before, until that conversation with Jaime.

Because she also needed to know what she was getting into, what baggage he was carrying and how it might bleed over.

Hell, most sane people would say that his life for the past decade was a giant red flag, littered as it was with lost friendships and relationships that had never gotten off the ground because half of their party—him—had quite literally flown away whenever he got the whim.

But Heidi needed to know that he didn't have the whim now, and that when he did travel, he wanted it to be with her by his side.

And how was she going to believe that, huh, genius?

He'd been back for all of a month, had spent even less time than that with her. Why would she think that anything about him had changed or *would* change or—

She placed her hand on his thigh, making him jump and lurch away from the contact. Because he wanted to move closer. *Fuck.* His breath sawed in and out. His—

"D-do—"

The word was tentative enough that his eyes flew from the ground, from where he'd been counting the grains in the piece of hardwood floor at his feet, up to hers, up to collide with tentative hazel eyes that socked him in the gut.

"Do what?" he asked.

Pink on her cheeks, her eyes darting away. "Do you not . . ." A sigh before her chin rose. "Do you not want me that way?"

# EIGHTEEN

Heidi

"*WHAT?*" he roared, closing the distance between them and all but hauling her into his lap. He grabbed her hand, brought it toward his hips, pressing it firmly against the hard length of his erection.

Her fingers convulsed instinctively, wrapping around his cock as much as they were able through the fabric of his jeans.

He groaned, dropped his forehead to hers. "*That's* how much I want you. You breathe, and I'm hard. You smile, and I'm aching. You laugh and I'm ready to tear your clothes off."

"But . . ." she whispered.

"But what?"

Embarrassment flooded through her, but she had to know, had to make sure that she hadn't imagined . . . well, hadn't made things bigger in her head than they were in real life. "But . . . things were just getting good, and then you stopped."

Brad froze.

Then he grinned, a hot, slow smile that she felt trickle along every nerve ending.

"What?" she asked.

The pale lighting brought out the golden hues hidden in his deep brown hair, made the stubble on his cheeks seem even darker. But it was his eyes that held her in place, that made her heart skip a beat.

He stood, bringing her with him, then walked toward the headboard, positioning them both so they were resting with their backs against it.

Or rather, *he* had his back against it.

She was able to relax in the enviable circle of his arms, sitting on his lap, her shoulder against his chest, but best of all was the way his arms wrapped around her, drawing her close to his body, holding her tightly. She was protected, cared for, held as though she were important.

"Okay," he said. "I'm only going to say this once." He paused, waited until her gaze came to his. "You are quite literally the woman that I want most in this world. And I've been to a shit-ton of places," he added, tucking a strand of hair behind her ear. "So you can know that I'm not spouting bullshit. Also, by want, I mean sexually. Refer back to all that breathing, smiling, laughing, and my cock feeling like it's going to break in half stuff I mentioned previously."

His fingers brushed the shell of her ear, making her shiver and drift closer, until she could feel his next words glaze her lips. "But, also, more importantly, by want, I mean I can honestly say that you are the first woman I've ever spent time with who's made me look inside and recognize that I have some shitty characteristics that I need to change."

She frowned, but he dropped a finger to her lips before she could protest.

"I hurt you," he whispered, his tone making her lungs seize, her heart convulse because there was so much pain in those words, "and I will regret doing that for the rest of my life."

"I'm okay," she whispered.

He smiled gently. "Of course, you are. Because you're smart and capable and beautiful, and you don't let dumbasses like me ruin your groove."

Laughter bubbled up in her chest, but she held it back. "That's true," she said instead, keeping her tone light.

"But," he said. "I *did* hurt you, and I hate that I did, and"—a sharp sigh—"well, the truth is that I didn't even understand *why* I'd done it, why I'd panicked and run until two weeks ago."

She rested her hand on his shoulder, kneaded the tight muscles there. "Why did you panic and run?"

"Because you were different."

Maybe the words should have hurt her feelings—being different wasn't typically good in these scenarios—but instead, she understood at least part of what he was saying.

Because he'd been different, too.

"Baby," she whispered.

"No," he said. "Just let me get this out, okay? And then you can decide if you're going to walk out that door, like I probably deserve, or . . ."

"Or what?" she asked after a few moments when he hadn't finished the thought.

"Or"—his hands came to her jaw, cupping it gently—"if you'll let me keep you forever."

Her pulse had slowed from the frenzied tattoo of their kissing, a steady and calm *thrum-thrum, thrum-thrum, thrum-thrum* that was pumping blood evenly through her veins. But his words sent it into warp speed, carousing through her body, vibrating in her fingertips, galloping through her legs, whirling through her brain.

"For-forever?"

Gentle, still so gentle, but his eyes, they held a touch of humor. "Yes," he said. "Forever. That's what people do when they find the one person on this planet who's destined for them above all others."

That almost poetry sang to a part of her—the piece that had been devastated when she'd woken alone that day only a few months before, the same piece that understood what he was saying, that felt the same, that wanted that *forever*.

The rest of her . . . was overwhelmed.

She hardly knew this man.

But . . . was that really accurate?

True, they hadn't logged a lot of hours together yet, but she had seen so many of the important things. His time with Stef, the books, the date, the dinners and ice cream and movies and bad reality TV. The way he made her laugh and was quick to do so at himself. He was a good man—she knew that in her bones, knew it with as much certainty as she understood how many electrons orbited an atom of helium (that being two).

She'd already decided she wasn't a coward.

She'd already decided she was going to see where things went with this man.

So, why couldn't it be forever?

Why not her? Why not this wonderful man?

With the sun long set, with neighbors overhead clomping noisily across the ceiling, with a lovely, funny, sexy man in front of her, saying he wanted her . . . why couldn't that be?

There wasn't any reason.

It *could* be.

Heart still tripping along, her pulse still skittering in her veins, she peeled his hands from her cheeks, lacing their fingers together. "Okay," she murmured. "What do you need to tell me?"

What could this man possibly tell her that he thought might have her bolting for the door?

His eyes were equal parts wary and concerned.

"I keep people at a distance, so they can't leave me." He swallowed hard. "So they can't hurt me."

She waited.

Because clearly, there must be more to this.

"I've done it since I was a kid," he said. "I didn't really realize it until recently, but I think it started when my mom got sick. It was easier to pretend everything was fine, that *I* was fine." He sighed. "But the truth is that I continued doing it, and I used traveling as an excuse to keep my distance even more."

She squeezed his hands. "Hard to have a serious relationship when you're out of the country all the time."

"Yes. That."

"I'm sorry your mom was sick," she said.

His eyes softened. "It was a long time ago."

"She's a big presence in your guys' lives, though." Heidi slipped one hand free so she could push back her hair that seemed determined to get into her eyes. "I can tell that just from the couple of times I've met her."

"She is," he told her. "She's the glue that holds everything together."

"I can see how the fear of losing that might affect you."

Brad stilled. "Why am I hearing a but?"

She winced. "Well, it's not so much a but—"

He cursed. "I get it," he said, interrupting her and taking off down a tangent that had nothing to do with anything that she'd been thinking. "I understand why you wouldn't want to trust your heart with someone who's just going to flit off and leave you alone—someone who's *already* done that. I totally get it if you want me to just keep my distance, to not keep pursuing you. Hell, if I was in your position, I wouldn't have been nearly as nice or understanding as you've been. I would have kicked my ass to the curb and—"

"Are you?" she interrupted, having the feeling that if she

*didn't* interrupt, then she might never get another word in edgewise. He was too far along the road of self-chastisement, determined to flagellate himself until he was sufficiently punished for his transgressions.

She saw now.

She understood now. What was in her heart . . . and what was in his.

Beyond the courage she'd summoned to take a chance with him, beyond her own hang-ups with self-worth, she saw that this man would take every opportunity to carry more than his fair share of burdens. He'd continue taking them on, one after another, piling them across his shoulders until he couldn't take a step, couldn't move forward at all.

Unless she stopped him.

His words had faltered at her question, but he didn't answer it.

So, she prompted him again. "Are you?"

He blinked. "Am I what?"

"Are you going to flit off and leave me to wake up in my bed all alone again?"

His expression clouded. "Fuck, no," he said. "I've spent the last months imagining all the places I want to take you, everything I want you to see. If I travel, I want you right by my side."

"So, that's it?"

Brows drawing together, he cocked his head to the side. "What do you mean?"

"Is that all of your baggage? Everything that would have me kicking you to the proverbial curb?"

"I—um—I—" His mouth opened and closed a few times, sounds rumbling up from his throat but not coalescing into actual words.

She took pity on him. "I get keeping people at a distance, honey. I have a fucking PhD in the subject myself. My parents .

. . well, my dad is great, if sometimes a bit distant, and my mom . . . she's not so great, even though I keep telling myself that she always means well. It's just . . . she's not like your mom, and she's given me some wounds that run deep. So trusting people doesn't come easily for me. So I might push you away to stay safe." She trailed the fingers of her free hand along his jaw. "The thing is you say you've used avoiding connections like a shield. And I get that. I *feel* that sentiment in my bones. I've had my heart broken, have that baggage with my mom, and those hurts, they fucking suck." She swallowed. "But when I saw how happy Kate was with Jaime, when I saw the relationship Kels has with Tanner, I knew that I wanted that."

She rested her palm on his chest, feeling the steady beat of his heart beneath. "I was fucking terrified to take that first step, to even *admit* that what I had in my life wasn't enough, but I did it. I promised myself that I would try, would hold tight to the truth that I was worth finding something as special as they had, and I *did* find it." Smiling up at him, she said, "Also newsflash, what I found was you."

He inhaled sharply.

She pressed a kiss to his lips. "Because you're good and smart and caring and so much more than I could have hoped for, even with that armor on. But you know what's better?"

He shook his head.

"I think we've both come to the conclusion that whatever this is between us is different, is *more*. That it has the potential to be what Kate and Jaime have, what Kels and Tanner do, too."

She released a breath, laid the resolution she'd come to just before calling Kate and waking her friend up in the middle of the night on her honeymoon, who'd then had to wake up Jaime to get Brad's address, on the table (also, yes, she knew that she'd rung the alarm at the gossip committee and that her friends and all their nosiness would be descending shortly . . . but also, she didn't care, because Brad was important. Maybe it was some-thing in the Huntington gene pool, maybe it was just the power of Brad himself . . . or maybe she was digressing when she really should be focusing on telling this man what was in her heart).

"So what I'm trying to tell you is to bring that armor, carry that big ass shield, try to keep me at a distance because I won't stay away. Because . . . my armor is gone," she said. "Or maybe when it came to you, honey, I never had any."

He was still as a statue, hardly breathing, his eyes locked on hers.

Meanwhile, she was breathing heavily, her heart pounding, her lungs working hard after that long-ass speech.

And he was frozen, shock written into every line of his face.

"Did I break you?" she asked, jostling his chest lightly.

Her question seemed to snap him out of whatever trance he'd stumbled into, because he blinked, his hand slipped from hers, his arms banded around her, and he drew her flush against him. "No," he whispered. "You didn't break me. You turned the key, made me see exactly what I was missing."

Her heart pulsed, happiness welling within her. "Great," she said, wrapping her arms around him in turn, bringing their mouths close so the barest millimeter separated them. "So now, will you get back to kissing me?"

She had one quick glimpse of that slow, sexy smile of his, the one that always melted her from the inside out.

Then his mouth was on hers.

# NINETEEN

Brad

KISSING.

It was all back to kissing.

Only this time, it was without the cloud hanging over him, the tendrils of dread in his gut. He was able to just be in this moment with the woman he loved and really fucking enjoy kissing the hell out of her.

There was no hesitation in their touches, in the strokes of their tongues.

They'd gotten that all out of their systems months ago. Tonight was about leaning into those caresses, holding tight to the passion, embracing the need that made his hands shake and sweat break out on his back. It was about remembering every single thing that had made this woman moan, her breathing hitch, her eyes glaze over in desire.

And then he was doing them all on repeat.

One quick movement had their positions reversed and moved down on the bed, her head hitting the pillow, her back on the mattress, her body sprawled out beneath him.

Then he was kissing her again, stroking his tongue along the seam of her lips, tasting the mix of sweet and tart that was only Heidi. She opened, and their tongues collided, waltzing around each other, a frenzy of movements that had him groaning into her mouth.

But his hands weren't stationary. They were busy, remembering every curve, slipping beneath the fabric of her sweatshirt and finding the hot skin beneath. Her breathing hitched when he traced up and over her rib cage, before that hiccup of air turned into a soft, low moan that had his blood going molten. He traced higher, slipping beneath the band of her bra, fingers grazing the underside of one breast before moving to the other in a steady back and forth that had her head falling back on the pillows, their lips pulling apart.

He didn't want to stop kissing her, didn't want to lose that taste on his tongue.

But he supposed there were plenty of other places demanding to be kissed, beginning with the hardened tip of her nipple that was beading against the fabric of her bra, poking through the lace to press against his palm when he cupped one breast lightly.

Dragging his mouth down her neck, he tasted the salt mixing with sweet and spice and tart, soaking it in as he made his way to the zipper at the top of her hoodie, tugging it down, the *zip* loud in the quiet of the room only punctuated by rapid breaths and the occasional *thunk* from his loud ass neighbors overhead. Knowing he'd never get to kiss and touch like he wanted without removing it, he coaxed the sweatshirt down her arms, tossed it to the side, and then stared down at this woman, at his beautiful Heidi—

Who was wearing a T-shirt that said, *I Make Bad Science Puns . . . Periodically.*

And he laughed.

Because she was different. Because she was funny. Because she was just so . . . Heidi.

"What is it?" she asked, reaching for his shoulders.

He smoothed his hand over her cheek, down her arm, along her torso, and stopped, slipping it under the hem of her shirt to rest on the warm heat of her abdomen.

"You're just so fucking perfect for me."

Her eyes widened, lips parting, and he couldn't resist one more taste of that mouth, enticing her into a heated kiss that had them both gasping, and at least for him, his vision edged in black by the time he managed to tear himself away. But though he left her to draw in a breath, he didn't remove his mouth from her body. Instead, he dragged it over her throat, dipped his tongue into the small hollow at the base of her neck, nipped lightly at her collarbones. Still, the fucking fabric of her shirt impeded him, so he managed to pull himself away from her long enough to tug the cotton over her head, to toss it somewhere in the vicinity of her hoodie.

But when he went to return his mouth to her skin, bent on kissing every inch, she placed her hand on his chest, stilling him.

His eyes met hers.

"Naked first," she said.

Well, now. He could work with that.

His fingers went to work on her pajamas, tugging them off her legs and dragging her underwear down along with them. Those two went by the wayside, and a heartbeat later, he'd slipped a hand beneath her, undoing her bra and peeling the pale pink lace away.

Naked.

Yes. So much better.

But when he went to crawl back on top of her, she stopped him again with her hand on his chest.

He glanced down, realized he'd forgotten her socks, and tugged those off as well.

But she halted him again before he could sink between her thighs.

"What?" he asked, mouth watering with the need to taste, fingers itching to touch.

Her color was high, her lips reddened and swollen from his kisses, but still her voice was steady when she ordered, "You need to be naked, too."

That was what he wanted.

That was also a big problem.

Because he wanted this woman quite desperately, and if *he* was naked, too, he might embarrass them both. Well, embarrass himself, and make her quite unhappy.

"Heidi," he began.

She shook her head, arms crossing beneath her breasts, plumping the mounds into a nearly irresistible temptation. "No, Brad. No dice. You get naked right now, or else this isn't happening."

"I—"

"I don't care if you're nearly at the end of your control, or if you want to enjoy me first, or whatever other bullshit man stuff you have flitting through that brain of yours." Her eyes flashed with irritation. "I need to be able to touch you, to feel your skin on my palms, to hold your body to mine without any barriers. Another time you can tease me until your heart's content." Her gaze softened. "But tonight, I need you to be right here with me."

He would have agreed, just because she asked.

But her giving him the words, telling him what was in her heart and mind . . . well, that absolutely slayed him.

And he knew in that moment, that he would never be able

to deny this woman anything. He'd been written into existence for her, just as she'd been made to fit him perfectly.

They had the potential to be like his brother and Kate.

No, they *would* be like his brother and Kate.

Minus the rooster and gaggle of animals.

Though, as he stood and methodically stripped off his clothes, letting them drop to the floor, he knew that just as he couldn't deny Heidi what she wanted, if she asked for a rooster, he'd buy the bird the fucking tuxedo himself.

A moment later, Fuzzy McFeatherston wasn't the cock he was thinking of. All his focus was diverted to the woman grabbing onto the cock swinging between his legs. The cock that was harder than he'd ever believed possible and throbbing with the need to spread Heidi's thighs and plunge deep.

Seemingly reading his mind, or at least the mind of the body part south of the border, she kept her grip tight, sliding it up and down the hard length of him. "Please say you have a condom," she murmured.

He was in the middle of biting back a groan, his hips thrusting forward, pleasure rolling down his spine in waves, when he realized what she'd asked.

What she'd asked.

And what he didn't have.

Fuck. *Fuck*.

The groan he'd bit back burst forth, startling her into opening her eyes, the hazel depths cloudy with need . . . and then sharpening as horror dawned. "You don't have a condom?"

He shook his head. "I've been meaning to pick some up, but I've been too busy with . . ."

She was shoving him off her, and for a moment, he thought he'd revealed the straw that had broken the camel's back. But then she was striding across the room, glorious ass bouncing as she stalked to her purse, which apparently had fallen near the couch, and scooping it up.

She strode back, and he was torn where to look—those bouncing breasts, lower to the neatly trimmed dark hair hiding the pussy he wanted to get his mouth on and his tongue inside, or to any of the tempting places in between. The trio of freckles beneath her right nipple, the star-shaped tattoo on her rib cage, the dainty dip of her belly button, the faint birthmark on her hip.

Hell, he would even be thrilled to put in quality time with her feet, with those cute little toes, their nails now painted in a bright pink, all except for the big toe, which had a tiny rendering of a palm tree.

A palm tree that was tapping just beneath his line of vision, Heidi having made her way back to stand by the bed.

She cleared her throat, and he forced his gaze to rise to hers, albeit taking a slow, meandering path up those strong and sensual legs, past the thighs he needed to lick his way up, beyond her stomach and ribs and even her breasts, though it lingered there long enough for her to clear her throat for a second time.

But then his eyes were on hers.

"Do women have to do *everything?*" she snapped, but her stare gave her away, warmth turning the grays and browns and greens of her eyes into a deep russet with streaks of gold, any anger having been edged out by amusement.

Out of the corner of his vision, he saw her wave her hand, and what she was holding finally captured his focus.

He reached for the plastic square—or probably, he lunged for it, so desperate he was to be inside her at this point—but she danced back, holding it out of reach. "Uh-uh," she said, wicked-ness creeping into her expression. She stepped forward again, pushed him back onto the mattress. "She who brings the condom gets to ride the prize."

"Heidi."

"No arguments."

He snagged a hand around her waist, yanked the condom out of her grip, and tore it open with his teeth. A second later, it was on his cock and he was lying back, tugging her over him, coaxing her down onto the hard length of him.

"I don't care if you're on top," he said, breaths coming in short, staccato bursts. "So long as I'm inside—*ah* . . ." Holy fuck, that was good, the hot, tight sheath of her slipping down over him. ". . . you."

She bottomed out, and they both groaned in satisfaction, in relief, in . . . coming home.

Then she began to move. With slow, deliberate strokes that told him she hadn't forgotten their night together, that she'd remembered everything that had sent his blood boiling, his pleasure skyrocketing. His eyes rolled back, hips jerking up to meet her movements, and the tiny semblance of control he managed to keep hold of poofed away.

Gone. Disappeared to God knew where.

He forgot his own name.

He forgot to breathe.

He forgot to do anything but catapult toward the edge of oblivion, doing everything in his power to bring this woman along with him as she rode him hard and fast, bringing his release forward far too quickly. He knew he wouldn't last long, knew he needed to get her there. She bucked against his thumb when he circled her clit, her thighs clenching tightly around him, her moans faltering and then breaking long and loud when he lurched up to suck a nipple deep.

But then her moans changed.

And she got close.

And then she was over.

*Thank fuck.*

Because then he was there, too.

And just like before, he knew he'd never be the same.

But *unlike* before, this time he didn't run.

He slept like a baby, holding the woman he loved in his arms, knowing that everything in his life would finally work out.

Only when he woke in the morning, it was to find that he might not have run.

But Heidi had.

# TWENTY

Heidi

SHE'D CLOSED her car door and rolled her shoulders, her brain absolute mush, but her heart completely full.

A night in Brad's arms.

A delicious orgasm, followed by a pair when he'd woken her in the middle of the night with fingers between her thighs and an urgent whisper of, "Please, tell me you have another condom."

In fact, she'd *had* another.

And the results had been . . . explosive.

So, when she'd gotten the call from Stef, asking if she might possibly have time to bring her computer to the hospital, she'd gone to her friend's apartment, gathered anything and everything Stef might need, including the laptop. She'd also inquired about Fred, the misbehaving pooch—who it turned out was safe in the care of Stef's dog sitter—and tried unsuccessfully to avoid the topic of Brad.

Not because she wanted to hide things.

Quite the opposite, actually. She was practically bubbling with joy and excitement and affection for the man.

But she wanted Brad to be *just* hers for a little while longer.

Then she'd do the adult thing and share.

Luckily, Stef's doctor had come in before the interrogation had gotten too intense, but Heidi knew it wouldn't be long before she got the fifth degree from multiple angles. Hell, Stef would probably join forces with Cora, Kate, and Kelsey and then it would be four against one.

And if she were being completely truthful, she *couldn't* wait to share her happiness with her friends.

She'd hoped to go back to Brad's afterward, to knock on his door—since he hadn't had a set of hooks in his apartment with a labeled spare for her to pilfer, like she had at her place—but then she'd gotten pulled into the lab to double-check the calibrations so the assistant staff could be confident running everything.

That was supposed to have been a short visit—her goal of getting back to Brad still within reach.

But after she'd checked the equipment, made sure everything was ready to roll without her, she had run into the head of operations.

And then she'd become mean boss.

Or mean underling, she supposed, since she didn't outrank him, though her lab was run outside of the normal management channels. Either way, she'd read him the riot act—professionally, of course—and by then the CEO had gotten word of what had nearly happened, and she ended up on a call with those two and the heads of the Health and Human Services and Occupational Health . . . and well, she didn't want to get the cleaning staff in trouble, per se. They worked hard, but the team needed to find out if it was a lack of training that had caused the crew to be where they shouldn't, or if it was because they were disregarding the protocols.

The details of how they sorted that out weren't important—and not part of her job, suffice to say—but Heidi was very confident there wouldn't be another issue.

Especially because as she'd left, she'd seen the keypad lock being installed on the door.

It would go into operation tomorrow, and *she* would be setting the codes.

Not quite a lock and key, but she'd take this version.

But now it was late in the afternoon, and she was back at her place after having stopped by to make sure Stef was good, but Heidi hadn't stayed long at the hospital. She was tired from her early morning and from lack of sleep the night before—though she couldn't complain about the cause of the latter—and all she wanted to do was change into some jammies and then call Brad.

Maybe she could convince him to bring pizza again.

"You just going to stand there all day?"

She jumped, whirled around, her elbow colliding with the car window, making her wince and rub the abused joint.

"Stop doing *that*," she hissed at Brad, who was closing the distance between them with a decidedly stormy expression, one that tempered the burst of excitement she'd felt at hearing his voice, at seeing him.

"At least you weren't near a hill you could fall down this time."

He stopped in front of her, crossed his arms.

"What?" she asked.

He just lifted a brow.

"*What?*" she asked again.

"You pulled a runner?" he asked. "Really?" He shifted closer, placing his hands on either side of her, boxing her in against her car, the spicy maleness of him wafting over her, the hard, hot lines of his body pressed to hers, causing her to need a minute to process his words. Which is probably why he continued talking. "You can run, Heidi. You can run from us, from me. You can put that armor back on, but I'm not letting you go. I'm not giving you up—not when what we have is so fucking—"

She was confused and tired, and her feet hurt from being on them for most of the day.

She wanted those jammies and that pizza . . . and this man.

Which was why she placed her fingers over his mouth and asked, "What the fuck are you talking about?" Of course, then she didn't give him a chance to answer, not when the first part of his words processed, and she'd finally comprehended what he'd said. "What the hell do you mean, I pulled a runner?" she snapped. "I came here and put on adult clothes, visited Stef in the hospital, was pulled into work, and then went back to see Stef, and now I came home to shower." She glared. "After which I was going to put on pajamas and see if I could convince you to bring me *pizza!*" She jabbed a finger into his chest. "How is that pulling a runner? How is that—"

"You left," he said, eyes hot with anger, body still pressed to hers, a growing situation against her abdomen, making her lose the threads on her outburst. "And you didn't pick up your phone." His fingers tangled in her hair. "And you weren't here. Weren't on the trail. I even called Jaime to see if Kate had heard from you because . . ."

"You'd thought I'd left," she finished.

He nodded, brows drawn together.

Any irritation she'd been feeling from his demeanor faded. Because she knew what that felt like, and further that, she knew what he'd revealed last night might not have seemed like a giant bombshell to her, but that it had been big to him, something that had eaten at him for a while.

Then to wake up and find her not there.

"Did you not see the note I left you?"

She'd tacked it right to the center of his mirror, thinking he wouldn't miss it, would stumble upon it first thing when he got up and . . . well, used the facilities.

His lips parted on an exhale.

"You didn't," she confirmed.

He shook his head, his expression drawn, his eyes downcast.

"Oh honey," she murmured, pushing lightly at his chest, coaxing him back a step, heart squeezing. "I told you last night, I'm not going anywhere." She took his hand, straightened her purse on her shoulder. "Come on. Let's go inside." Once they'd made it through the door, she asked, "Why didn't you call me?"

He turned and shut the wooden panel, flipping the lock. "I told you earlier," he said, though his tone was without rancor. "I did, but you didn't pick up."

Frowning, she slipped off her shoes, tucked them neatly on the rack, then hung her purse on its hook, reaching inside for her phone. "Oh." She winced. She'd turned it off when she went into the lab . . .

And hadn't turned it on.

Warm fingers covered hers, snagging her cell, and then Brad glanced down at the screen.

His eyes rose to hers, hazel irises darkened with frustration. "Seriously?"

She winced again. "It's not like I *try* to forget . . ."

A sigh lifted his shoulders, sending them south on the exhale, his chin tipping back, gaze going up to the ceiling.

"Plus, no one besides my mom ever really calls me. They always text, and then when I get a moment to check, I catch up." Her own shoulders were inching up toward her ears, defensiveness and guilt warring within her. It really was a bad habit—not to have it off at work—but to be unavailable because she'd forgotten to turn her cell on at other times. This wasn't even the first time that she'd heard this same complaint.

But her friends got it, and she normally wasn't sad to miss a call from her mother, listing all of her inadequacies when it came to being a proper woman who could provide her grand-children.

Plus, her friends all had the direct line to her lab, so they could get her that way if it was an emergency. Or sometimes they emailed, reminding her to check her messages. But Brad hadn't had any of those options . . . because she hadn't given them to him.

Shit.

"I'm sorry," she said, turning and taking the phone from him —which he'd powered up—and setting it on the cradle she had on the table to charge. Already the screen was filling with missed calls, voicemails, and text banners. Yet another wince. "Really, I'll get better, and . . ."

She gave him her other info—her work email and number, even the information for the front desk, in case it was an emer-gency and he couldn't get her the other ways.

Dutifully, he typed in the numbers and saved her email to his contacts.

But though the edginess in his expression had eased . . . he still wasn't his normal smiling self, and another bolt of guilt shot through her. She'd dampened the comfortable rapport they'd built, made him worry while she'd spent the day in peaceful happiness.

And now her normally sweet, teasing, lovely man was . . . diminished, shadows beneath his eyes, lines edging his lush, kissable mouth.

"I really am sorry," she whispered.

He closed his eyes, inhaled and exhaled slowly. "It's not—"

He shook his head. "It's not your fault, sweetheart. I just . . . it—"

She did what she would have wanted.

She stepped into his arms and hugged him tightly.

He wrapped his arms around her in return, burying his face in her hair and breathed in deeply, just holding her for a long, long time. Eventually, he loosened his hold, stepping back and cupping her cheek. "I'm okay now," he murmured. "Sorry, I freaked out."

"Don't apologize. I'm the one who's—"

"Don't apologize," he said, taking a page out of her book, smiling down at her.

"Did we just have our first real fight?" she asked.

"No," he said, cupping her jaw. "That was when you told me I wasn't washing the dishes correctly."

She frowned, felt her brows draw together. "When was that?"

"One night, last week."

"*Which* night?"

Now she caught a glimmer of humor in his eyes, felt that last little bit of guilt settle and drift away.

"Not telling you, if you don't remember." A smirk that made her want to kiss him.

Well, she could do that.

So she did, lifting up on tiptoe and pressing her mouth to his. His lips parted immediately, and she dipped inside, loving that she could hold and touch and kiss this man. That he'd somehow become hers, that she'd likewise become his.

"You're impossible, you know that?" she asked when they pulled apart for air.

"I'm *something*," he said, wrapping his hands around her hips and tugging her against him, against his hard cock, his lips finding hers.

"Did you buy condoms?" she asked, tearing her lips from his to suck in air.

He gave her that slow, wicked smirk. "What do you think?"

"I *think* that you're a man who's always prepared."

Hoisting her up, his mouth dropping to her neck, his tongue flicking out to taste the sensitive spot, he spoke against her skin. "That's the correct answer."

She laughed, tugged his head back up, and stole his lips in a searing kiss that left her heart pounding, her lungs burning for air. Then she nodded toward the bedroom. "Turns out I'm a little tired," she said. "Maybe you can show me the proper way to use my mattress?"

"Is that a thing?" he asked, already moving in that direction.

She dug her nails into his shoulders when he nipped at her earlobe, sending heat scorching through her body. Rotating her head, she did some nipping of her own. "If it gets you inside me sooner, then, yes, it is."

His eyes seared into hers, and she found herself on the bed a heartbeat later.

And it turned out, he *could* show her the proper way to use her mattress.

*Twice.*

# TWENTY-ONE

Brad

HE STARED at the woman who'd stolen his heart and smiled.

She was too fucking cute, her hair pulled back into a high ponytail, tight jeans encasing the sexy legs he'd spent a copious amount of time in between this last month. Her color was high from her exertion on the trail, but she hadn't once complained that he'd hauled her out of bed on a Saturday morning before sunrise and had driven her out to this regional park.

That had probably been helped by the hot coffee and two huge banana chocolate chip muffins he'd used to coax her out from beneath the covers.

Luckily for him, she was a morning person, and though she'd grumbled and groaned a little bit, she'd quickly gotten into the spirit of the adventure.

Now, they'd reached the precipice of that sharp incline and could see the view he'd known would be spectacular, but that was made even more so by Heidi being next to him.

She sank down onto a bench, and he plunked down next to

her, warning, "I'm all sweaty," when she cuddled up next to him.

"Well, I am, too," she said, wrapping an arm around his waist and snuggling her head into his chest. "Two sweaties make a right."

He laughed, but then the sun made it fully over the horizon behind them, its rays flying forward to glimmer over the ocean in front of them, making the moisture in the air sparkle like golden smoke, or maybe like some sort of otherworldly magical power. Lifting his camera, he took several shots of the gorgeous display. But then his focus—and the camera lens—drew back down, and he took pictures of Heidi.

Who, once she realized what he was doing, blushed and hid her face in his chest. "Close-up, much?" she said against his T-shirt.

He laughed but set the camera aside, cupping the side of her face and turning it up so he could kiss her. "Only way to capture those beautiful eyes of yours."

She made a face.

He kissed her.

But eventually, they needed air and broke apart, sitting on that bench, on a precipice high above civilization, looking out at the Pacific Ocean, and watching the sky brighten as the sun rose behind them.

He'd traveled the globe, visited all seven continents, stayed in tiny villages and big cities, and never had he felt more certain that he was in the right place.

Because the right person was next to him.

---

LATER THAT DAY, after they'd taken a much-deserved nap, they made plans to binge another of Heidi's bad reality TV shows—

and he wouldn't admit this to anyone, but he'd actually begun to like them . . . okay, *some* of them. But what he really liked was her reactions to them.

The gasps of outrage.

The anger for one of the cast being wronged—which usually came in the form of a broken heart.

The occasional tear when something sweet happened.

But just as they had pulled out their phones to figure out what to order in for dinner, there was a knock at the door.

Heidi frowned.

"I've got it," he told her, shifting her feet from his lap and standing up.

"It's probably someone trying to sell me solar panels," she grumbled.

"Well, I'll tell them to take a hike," he said, opening the door.

"That hike isn't happening, bro," his brother said, towering over a trio of women. He laughed, probably at the confusion on Brad's face when that trio pushed the door open, barreled past him with nary a look, and sandwiched themselves around Heidi on the couch.

"I haven't seen this episode," Kate said, grabbing the bowl of popcorn he'd made—and for the record, had only gotten to eat one handful of. "Start it over."

"Come on."

Brad blinked at Jaime's voice, blinked again when a jacket was shoved into his chest, followed by his wallet, keys, and phone—all of which had been given a proper home on Heidi's organization station by the door.

"Let's go."

"Go where?" he asked as Jaime threw his arm around his shoulders.

"Whatever you were planning with Heidi ain't happening."

He coaxed Brad out the door. "So, let's go grab a beer and some wings."

"I—" He shook his head. "What?"

Jaime sighed and started hauling Brad down the porch.

"Wait—" He ducked out from beneath his brother's arm, hopped up the stairs, and locked the door. Then turned back around to see Jaime studying him. "What?"

His brother just smiled and shook his head. "Let's go get that beer."

---

"Okay," Jaime said when they were seated at a bar with a scarred wooden top, their stools slanted so they could watch the latest Gold Hockey game.

"Okay, what?"

"Tell me *all* about it."

He took a sip of his beer. "About what?" he asked, playing dumb.

Jaime rolled his eyes. "Nice try. But we've been back a week, and Kate has been beside herself with curiosity. You need to give me the goods or my new wife will leave me."

Brad snorted. "Then she'd have to find someone to take care of the cock."

His brother froze, slowly set down his beer. "Dude."

"Heidi would have laughed," he muttered, glugging down his own, since Jaime had driven them to the bar.

"Heidi is actually why we're in this mess."

He glared. "Don't say anything bad about her. She's great."

Jaime raised his hands in surrender. "I would never do that. She *is* great, and she's one of Kate's best friends, but . . ." He trailed off, like Brad would fill in the blanks.

And he supposed he would.

Because he knew exactly what his brother was thinking.

When would he be leaving again?

Reaching across, he grabbed Jaime's forearm, squeezing it tightly—not because he wanted to hurt his brother, but because he needed him to understand. "She's it."

Jaime nodded, but concern was still laced throughout his expression, and Brad knew he didn't get it.

"She's my Kate," he said. "You know all that shit with Mom, with that grain of sand itching beneath the surface, the prickle of irritation that never seemed to go away?"

Jaime nodded when he paused.

"To keep with the metaphor, Heidi is that pearl."

Brad waited . . . and then waited some more for his brother to say something, to congratulate him on finding the other half of his soul, but Jaime just quietly stared at him.

"You're wondering if I'm just going to fucking disappear again, aren't you?" He pulled his hand back, clenched his jaw tight. "Well, I'm not. I've been all over this fucking world, and I can say with absolute certainty that none of that means anything without a person to share it with."

"So, does that mean you're done traveling, that you're just going to live here permanently?"

"Yes." He sighed when he saw his brother still didn't get it. And who could blame him?

Brad had taken a sharp right turn.

Hesitation in his brother's gaze, and fuck that stung. "I don't think you would hurt her intentionally," Jaime began. "But I wonder . . . if you're not moving kind of quickly. You're used to being free and moving to your own beat all the time." He lifted his hands, palms out in surrender. "I'm not saying that's a bad thing, not at all. I just . . . I know that Heidi is married to her job here, and she has deep roots in this area. She grew up here. Cora, Kelsey, and Kate are here. I'm sure she'd be happy to travel—I've never seen that woman back down from an adventure or a challenge, but I don't think that she'd be happy to uproot her life all the time." He winced. "And frankly, I don't think her job will allow for it."

None of these were things Brad didn't know.

But none of these things made that old prickling to run, to leave, to hide beneath the prospect of leaving, come back.

Instead, he just felt certain.

That he'd be putting down his roots where Heidi was.

"Look, Jaim, I know what you're saying." He sighed. "But the truth is that for the first time in my life, I don't have another trip planned. Usually, when I'm still in the middle of one set of travels, I'm already searching for the next place to visit, chasing that high of something new, something that could mute the itch that tells me to keep moving, to keep searching, to never stop looking." He clenched his hand into a fist, rested it on his thigh. "This is different. I *feel* different."

"How?"

"When I first met Heidi, it was like everything inside me both stood up at attention and settled down. I knew that she was special, but I was fucking terrified after spending time with her. I knew that given the chance, she'd burrow herself deep inside my soul, and not because she was trying to, but because she *didn't have to*." A shake of his head. "She was just herself, and I knew that she was more than anyone I had ever met. She's fucking incredible, and she was in me deep in an instant . . . and I was so unnerved that I ran in the other direction."

Jaime was quiet for a moment then asked, "What changed now?"

He stopped, considered how he could possibly encapsulate how *much* had changed.

Because *everything* had changed.

"Jaime," he began. "There's . . ." Then stalled out.

"Hey." His brother grabbed his shoulder, squeezing it lightly until Brad looked up from counting the bubbles in the froth of his beer. "The girls are together and watching reality TV. They've got a bottle of tequila for margaritas, books to discuss, and two members of their Un-Wine Club to interrogate —Heidi, because of you, and Kate, about our honeymoon." He picked up Brad's beer and handed it to him before snagging his own and *clinking* the glasses together. "What I'm trying to say is that we have plenty of time to hash out all this shit." He took a sip. "It'll be a good four hours before I get the call to go play designated driver."

Brad traced a pattern in the condensation on the outside of his glass.

"I know it seems like I'm being an asshole," Jaime said, "and it's not that I don't believe what you're saying. I'm just—I don't want either of you hurt, and I don't want you to have gotten things straight in your head and then limit yourself and—*fuck*, now I sound like an extra-large asshole." He thumped his hand on the bar. "Ignore me. I'm playing the role of the worried older brother. You're great. Heidi is great. You both deserve to be happy, regardless of my big brother vibes."

"Jaim," he said and stopped, not sure what to say, not when his mind was spinning.

"Fuck," Jaime said, probably catching a glimpse of that whirlwind. He shoved a hand into his hair. "*For real.* Ignore me. I don't have any right to question you or Heidi's decisions. You know that my relationship with Kate all began with a lie. We pretended to be engaged, for fuck's sake, so how could I possibly think that I can give anyone any advice on relationships?"

Brad's shoulders relaxed, the tension in his gut brought on by his brother's questions easing with the sincerity in his tone.

"If Heidi is *your* Kate, then I'm so fucking happy for you." Jaime laughed. "Because God knows these women give us a hell of a ride. But it's absolutely worth it, and I thank *fuck* every single day that I answered that DM, that I somehow managed to get Kate in my life."

"And now she's tied to you permanently," he said.

Jaime nodded, happiness etched into the lines of his face. "Yup. She's mine forever."

A fact that made Brad very jealous.

He wanted Heidi in his life always. He wanted her to wear his ring, to carry his babies, to be tied to him forever.

Jaime chuckled. "Until she realizes that I did a shit job of collecting her gossip."

That made him smile and shake his head. "We'd do anything for them, wouldn't we?"

Jaime clinked their glasses again. "Yes, we would."

And with that, he took another sip, then a deep breath, and he told his brother everything—how his last trip had opened that lid and made him understand he wasn't happy, how coming back and realizing he'd hurt Heidi had made him feel like the lowest piece of shit on the planet, how Jaime telling him what their mom had said had made everything clear, how Heidi deciding to give him a chance had made everything seem possible, and how this last month had been the absolute best of his life.

He confessed every last thing in his heart and mind.

Because his brother *was* that older, constantly worrying sibling.

Because he wanted to tell someone who would understand, someone who got just how important this all was.

And because . . . he didn't want his brother to get in trouble with his wife.

*Heh.*

# TWENTY-TWO

Heidi

"I'M INVITING MY FRIEND, Stef, to join us on our next girl's night," she declared, the moment the door had shut behind the boys.

There was a strategy with these . . . playdates, she supposed was the correct word. But the point was, the person with all the gossip couldn't just give it up right away, she had to make the others work for it—

No. That wasn't true.

She wanted to share every detail with them.

Just first, she had the more pressing business of making sure Stef was included.

Cora sat back, snagging the bowl of popcorn from Kate's hands and scarfing down a huge handful. "Isn't she your assistant at work?"

"She's my lab assistant," Heidi told her. "Not answering my emails and taking notes during meetings. She runs the lab when I'm not there, and she just broke up with her boyfriend—who got her friends in the divorce, by the way, the fucking assholes—and she doesn't have any family close."

They all made sympathetic noises, lamenting about fair-weather friends, and she knew that Stef would be welcomed into the fold of the Un-Wine Club.

Kelsey grabbed Heidi's cell from the table, held it out to her. "Why don't you call her and invite her over?"

"Well, because her relationship isn't the only thing broken." Then she related the tale of Stef's dog and the broken ankle and the surgery. "She's been home for a bit now, but she's not up for traveling much yet."

"Oh my God," Kelsey said. "Poor thing."

Kate lifted her glass, already filled with a slushie margarita, courtesy of Cora having commandeered Heidi's blender and getting busy with the tequila, and took a huge sip. "Next time, we bring the party to her."

Cora nodded. "Totally agree. She won't know what hit her."

Kels grinned. "Exactly. We're like the mafia. Once you're in, there's no getting out."

Heidi relaxed, knowing that Stef would be right at home with her crew.

"What does she nerd out about?"

"You know," she said slowly. "I don't actually know."

Kate rubbed her hands together, evil-genius style. "We'll ply her with tequila and find out all of the deep and dirty secrets. Muahaha!"

"You're still high from your honeymoon," Cora said, shoving Kate's shoulder.

"Maybe." Kate shrugged, a smug smile on her lips. "Maybe not."

They laughed, and then Kelsey asked about the resort, and Kate was off and running, talking about all the fun things she and Jaime had done—from parasailing to massages on the beach, they seemed to have hit all that the hotel had to offer.

"But mostly," Kate said. "Mostly we had lots and lots of hot, monkey sex"—she reclined back on the couch—"and it was *glorious*."

They all made the appropriate sounds of retching and, "Oh God, my ears!"

But they were happy for Kate, happy that their friend had found the person she was supposed to spend the rest of her life with.

And then their eyes turned to her.

"What?" she asked innocently, taking a long sip of her drink.

Which Cora promptly snatched from her, making her nearly choke on the slush she'd managed to get in her mouth.

"Details." Kate bounced on the cushions next to her, cheeks highlighted pink from the power of tequila. "Now."

Heidi thought about drawing it out, about torturing her friends, getting them to beg for details. But in the end, she couldn't, and she didn't want to, and hell, she was fighting back the urge to yell from the rooftops that she loved one Brad Huntington.

Loved?

She froze, words screeching to a halt inside her throat.

Because loved?

A blip as her heart began beating again, as surety slid through her.

Yes. *Loved.*

She loved Brad.

And she was so fucking excited about it.

So she told her friends about falling in the creek, and the dinners and the dates, she told them about coffee and muffins and pre-dawn hikes. She told them about books and keys and a man who cared where she was.

But the *only* thing she didn't tell them was about the whole loving thing.

Because she was going to tell that to Brad first.

---

"MARGARITAS ARE THE BEST," she said, curling up on the couch and resting her head on Kate's shoulder.

Kate tapped her glass against Heidi's. "I totally agree."

"Shh!" Cora hissed. "This is the best part!"

Dutifully, they both turned their gazes toward the TV, toward the knockdown, drag-out fight happening on the screen, then to their friend who was riveted by the action.

"You wouldn't be shushing us if you hadn't cheated and watched ahead," Heidi muttered grumpily.

"If I hadn't cheated and watched ahead, you would be missing this gloriousness right now," Cora pointed out.

Rightly so.

Which was why Heidi didn't argue, just put her glass to her lips and enjoyed the rest of her fourth margarita . . . or maybe it was her fifth? Lightweight that she was, she couldn't remember anything after the second. Mentally shrugging, she decided she didn't care. She could kick her friends to the curb, collapse into bed, and sleep until noon tomorrow if she wanted.

A table overturned on screen, sending an arrangement of cupcakes flying in all directions—and making her wince in memory of Kate's ruined wedding cake—but then she couldn't help but giggle.

Because the show's stars had decided to attempt to save the remaining stack that was teetering this way and that. Unfortunately for them, that teetering ended up turning into splatting when two of the cast slipped on fluorescent blue frosting and managed to knock the remainder of the sweet confections to the ground.

"You should take lessons from them," Kelsey said, her color high, the words carefully enunciated in a way that told Heidi she'd had more than three margaritas, too.

"Why?" she asked innocently. "It's not like there are any weddings coming up for me to ruin."

Kelsey took a sip. "Well, actually. Tanner and I did a thing."

She held up her hand.

Heidi squinted through blurry vision, blinking until it focused . . . on the sparkling diamond band sitting next to the engagement ring on Kelsey's finger.

Kate, the only one of them who had any skill in holding her alcohol, lurched up from the couch, nearly spilling the remnants of her margarita as she plunked the glass on the table and clambered over Cora's legs to grab Kels's hand.

"Are you fucking serious?" Cora asked, but it wasn't directed at Kate and her clambering.

Rather, it was said to Kels.

Who they all waited with baited breath to answer.

Who . . . nodded, her lips curving into a huge smile. "We eloped," she said. "We just . . . wanted to be married without all the hoopla." She nibbled on her bottom lip. "I was hoping you guys might be able to help us plan a big party to celebrate."

Heidi looked at Kate, who looked at Cora.

Then they all moved at once.

"Oh my God!" They all jumped up, throwing their arms around each other, a tequila-scented hug surrounding them all, their voices overlapping, the chatter indecipherable except that it was filled with excitement.

"When did you guys do it?" Kate asked once they'd

managed to calm themselves enough to conduct actual adult conversation again.

"Last weekend. We just woke up on Saturday morning and decided to fly to Vegas," Kels said, dutifully holding out her hand so they could admire the ring and then told them the rest of the story—how her family was pressuring her for a wedding (preferably a big one since Kels was the only daughter), how the wedding planning was stressing them out, and how they'd ultimately just decided to fly to Vegas and become husband and wife in truth. "I did promise my mom a big party," she said. "After we got home."

"Kels," Heidi whispered, hugging her tight. "I'm so happy for you."

Cora nudged her out of the way. "I need to hug the bride."

"Or the former one anyway. Now I'm just the wife," Kels said, her smile huge as she wrapped her arms about the petite brunette for a few moments before they all circled up, drinks in hand, and toasted Kels.

"Thank you, guys, but actually I feel terrible," she told them, setting her glass down then lifting her hands to her cheeks and pressing them against the flushed skin. "I think my mom is really disappointed."

Cora grinned. "She'll have a big party to plan. She'll be fine."

"You deserve to have what you want," Kate reminded her. "You didn't want a huge wedding with you at the center of it. You wanted your special moment with Tanner."

"You're not mad I didn't invite you guys?"

Heidi smoothed back her hair. "No, babe. We're happy that you're happy."

"You sure?"

Cora snorted and refilled her glass. "We're sure." A beat. "Just keep the cake far away from Heidi."

"Hey!"

Kels sank back down onto the couch, picking up her glass again and drinking deeply, her eyes still tinged with chagrin. "Even my mom and you guys aside, and the requisite guilt, it was still the happiest moment of my life." A sigh. "I love him so much, guys."

"Why am I sensing a but?"

Kels made a face. "Well, he had somehow taken the time to write these beautiful, touching vows, words that made my heart squeeze and my tears coming into my eyes and he'd probably been planning them for months, and I didn't even have anything besides the normal ones, and I kept thinking I should have done more."

Cora snorted. "Kels. Seriously?"

"What?" She tossed up her hands, nearly spilling her drink.

"He was just probably relieved he didn't have to keep waiting forever to marry you," Kate said. "Jaime told me that was the worst part of getting engaged . . . well, our real engagement anyway. That there was so much waiting until our real lives could start—not that we didn't have something real together before the wedding. It was just like there was a hidden hurdle ahead that we needed to leap over, and it didn't matter what flowers we had or the cake or the vows, we were just ready to start our happily ever after." She squeezed Kels's hand. "This is the important part. The rest of it is just . . . calorie-adding condiments to the happy sandwich of your lives."

Cora burst out laughing.

"What?" Kate asked on a scowl.

"Condiments?" Cora asked. "Really? What's the wedding? Mayonnaise?"

"Ew," Kate said. "No, it's fig jelly on a yummy toasted sourdough."

"What about apricot . . ."

Ignoring them waxing poetic about jam, Heidi gave Kels a squeeze. "I promise the vows aren't even registering in Tanner's brain at all."

"Even though mine were really freaking lame?"

"Even though."

Except . . . it wasn't Heidi replying.

They jumped, their gazes all shot to the door, noticing the three men standing in the hall, Brad closing the door behind them. Tanner, who'd been on a night shoot earlier and who also looked gorgeously rumpled, moved forward, closing the distance between him and Kels and pulling her into his arms. His lips went to her ear, and Heidi deliberately looked away after she heard, "I don't care, sweetheart. I just am so happy to be married to you, and I want to make babies and—"

Cora glared at Kate's hubby, talking over the lovey-dovey couple. "How long have you been there?"

"Since the squeeing," Jaime said dryly, slipping past her to kiss Kate soundly on her lips. "Thank God, Heidi has thick walls," he added when they'd broken apart for air. "Or else the neighbors would be complaining."

"I'll have you know," Heidi told him, though her eyes were on Brad, her gaze invariably drawn to his. "That I had the sheetrock sound-proofed for precisely that reason." She nibbled the inside of her mouth, stare dipping down to trace the yumminess that was the man who'd stolen her heart.

He was slender and muscled, the scruff on his jaw making her shiver in memory of how it had felt against her skin, her breasts, her thighs. But it was his eyes that truly drew her in. Because he looked at her just like Jaime looked at Kate, Tanner at Kels. With warmth and love and affection, and his own special brand of lighthearted Brad teasing.

One that made her smile, even now.

"Hi," he mouthed.

"Hi," she mouthed back.

His lips twitched.

Her heart thudded. The man was just wearing jeans, a T-shirt, socks, but he was still the most beautiful thing she had ever laid eyes on. Or maybe that was the way he made her feel.

Her gaze dropped down to his feet. To the socked feet.

Socked because he'd put his shoes on the rack.

Without a word from her, he'd noticed that she'd cleared a spot for him on the holder, and she hadn't even needed to mention it before he put his shoes there. He'd just paid attention and accepted that she liked things to be put in their proper spot. And he'd done it without comment.

And that, combined with the excitement of Kelsey, of her early morning with him, of the last few weeks and all his wonderfulness . . . and also maybe the margaritas—five, it was definitely *five*—had her blurting, "I love you!"

His eyes widened.

But she was more aware of the room going silent.

It *had* been filled with chatter, Cora, Kate, and Kels talking with Jaime and Tanner, but her blurt—okay, her yelled-out declaration—had the room going quiet, had five pairs of eyes coming to her. Well, six if she counted Brad, whose pretty hazel eyes were heavy with an emotion she couldn't read from this far away.

Then he was moving toward her.

More than moving toward her. One moment he was across the room, and the next he was *there*, one arm wrapping tightly around her hips and tugging her against his chest, the other moving higher, until his fingers slid in her hair, weaving into the strands and gently tilting her head back. "What did you say?" he whispered.

Kate's voice penetrated the Brad-fog descending around her. "We'll just go—"

"No," Cora said. "We're staying and—*ouch! Kels, let go!*"

And that was the last she heard of her friends—at least of any words being spoken, because obliquely, she processed them gathering their things, of footsteps moving toward the door, of that panel *clicking* closed behind them.

Then her condo was empty of everyone except her and Brad.

Who was stroking tiny circles on her scalp, making prickles of sensation trail down her spine, her arms.

"You love me?" he asked.

Her cheeks went hot—and not from the margaritas this time. The tequila was wearing off, and she was feeling exceptionally vulnerable, especially since. He. Hadn't. Said. It. Back.

"Brad," she whispered. "You . . . um—" She shook her head, dislodging his fingers, starting to pull away.

His arm around her waist tightened. "You love me?" he repeated.

"I—"

Not. A. Coward.

She lifted her chin. "Yes."

Joy in those hazel eyes, and then his mouth was on hers. He kissed her with an intensity that immediately had her pulse skittering, her heart squeezing tight.

Then just as abruptly pulled back.

"Wait," he said, breath coming in rapid gusts. "Are you too drunk to consent to this?"

"Too"—she blinked—"um . . . what?"

"Baby." He smoothed back her hair. "Jaime said you were drinking. Are you too drunk to—"

Her heart exploded.

Well, not literally, of course, but for a moment she was frozen in place, unable to believe that she could feel this much for another person. The only caveat, the single thing that crept into that joy, that weighed down her happiness, was that he hadn't said it back. Maybe it was too soon . . . or maybe it was too much.

Her gut clenched. That bliss was tempered by old insecurities.

Maybe she was destined to be a woman—like her mother had always said—who would end up alone without a person to love her for who she was inside. Maybe she worked too much, was too difficult.

Hell, maybe he'd come across her *Twilight* collection and had decided that was just a step too far.

Which would certainly put a damper on her feelings for this man.

"I'm not too drunk," she whispered, tugging at his arm, now feeling sick instead of joyful.

"You sure?"

She nodded, her gaze fixed on a spot over his shoulder when he didn't release her.

"What's the matter?"

He was honestly asking her what was the matter? She'd blurted out a huge freaking revelation in front of almost everyone who was important to her, and he had hardly acknowledged she'd told him she loved him, aside from confirming she'd said it in the first place.

Her eyes narrowed, and she opened her mouth.

Then froze when she realized he was slowly and inexorably leading her toward—

"Will you *stop* pushing me around?" she muttered, yanking at his arm.

"No," he said.

And then he spun her around.

"What—"

He pointed to a piece of paper in the middle of her

command center, neatly written and held in place by four purple magnets, one on each corner.

Her jaw fell open.

"Is *that* what's the matter?" he whispered into her ear, making her shiver, making her melt back against him.

Because that note, written in sure, firm strokes, said, "I love you."

"How long has that been there?" she asked.

He turned her in his arms, cupped her cheek. "Since last night."

A shuddering breath. "Really?"

He nodded.

"You love me?"

Another nod.

"Really?"

His lips quirked up. "Really, really."

"Are you sure?"

Annoyance had those lips pressing flat, his eyes going serious. "Heidi," he warned.

She nibbled at the corner of her mouth. "It's just that you haven't said it." She nodded at the note. "I mean, writing it isn't the same as saying it, is it?"

He growled, swept her up in his arms. "I love you, Heidi Greene. I love you so much that it feels like my heart will explode with happiness when I'm with you." He kissed her briefly, but intensely enough to have her pulse ratcheting up. Then he broke away, his expression gentle. "I love you with every bit of my soul, and I'll love you until that soul is no longer in my body." His forehead dropped to hers. "I never thought it was possible to feel this way for another person—"

She laughed.

He frowned. "What is it?"

Lifting her arms, she wrapped them around his neck. "It's

only that I was just thinking the same. I don't know how you did it, honey, but somehow what I feel for you is more than I ever could have imagined." She slid a hand to his chest, placed it over his pounding heart. "And this . . . *mine* . . . it beats for you."

He went still. "Heidi."

"What?"

"Fuck, I love you."

She smiled, lifted up so her lips were just a hairsbreadth from his. "Guess what?"

Affection—no, love—so much fucking *love* in his eyes. "What?" he asked gently.

"I love you."

He grinned.

"Also"—closer now, so her lips brushed his with every word she spoke—"the answer to your previous question of whether or not I'm sober enough to consent is . . . yes, baby, I am."

"Yeah?"

A nod. "What about you?"

He frowned.

"Are you sober enough to consent to *my* attentions?"

"What do you think?"

She blinked, realized he'd brought her to the bedroom, and then she smiled. "I think—*oof!*" He dropped her onto the mattress. "I think," she said again, gasping as he came on top of her, all of those glorious muscles pressing into her, "you'll do fine."

A wicked gleam in his eyes, his mouth coming down on top of hers.

And then he showed her just how fine he could be.

# TWENTY-THREE

Brad

HE WAS JUST FINISHING up the last bit of design for the latest website when there was a knock on his apartment door.

His eyes flicked to the clock on his computer screen, saw it was past seven.

And blinked.

Because *shit*, it was past *seven*.

After quickly saving his work—a habit that had taken just one time of losing copious amounts of data to become engrained in him—he stood and hurried to the door.

Heidi was on the other side.

"Shit, Heid," he said. "Why didn't you call?"

"I *did* call." She smiled, lightly poked his chest. "But I think you pulled a me and turned off your phone."

Closing the door behind her after she'd come in, he went to the counter and picked up his cell. It was on. He'd just been so engrossed in what he was doing that he hadn't heard it go off. Grimacing, he set it back down. "I'm sorry, baby. I lost track of time." He snagged her hand, brought her close. "Let me grab my shoes, and then we can go meet your friends."

"*Our* friends."

He smiled at that then dropped a kiss to her forehead. "Not sure if my brother can be considered a friend when he tries to order me around all the time."

A well-placed nudge with her elbow. "That ordering gene must be engrained in the Huntington DNA because you're sure good at it."

He affected innocence. "I don't know what you're talking about."

She laughed, and just like every other time he saw her happy, he felt the jagged pieces settle inside him. He lived for that sound, for her joy, more than he'd ever thought possible. It had been a month since that night at her place, since she'd told him she loved him, and it had all been . . . bliss.

More hikes—though not predawn, per her request. They'd gone to dinner, to the movies. He'd convinced her to do another touristy thing and take a ride on a cable car—which they'd both enjoyed much more than Alcatraz, him especially so, since she'd gotten cold on that foggy morning and had cuddled close to him as the rattling streetcar went up and down the hilly streets of San Francisco. Last week, they'd driven down to Santa Cruz and visited some absolutely huge redwoods in the morning then had taken a very bumpy ride on an old wooden roller coaster in the afternoon. And just yesterday, Heidi had taken the day off from the lab, and they'd driven a few hours north to a tiny lighthouse perched above a beach filled with sea glass.

And in between, they'd spent almost every night together, with the odd girl's night thrown in. On those evenings, he'd hung with Jaime, with Tanner, and occasionally, with a few of Tanner's friends, Sebastian and Devon Scott. The brothers were cool guys, and the tech worker and former hockey player, respectively, had nicely rounded out the group when they'd brought Max Montgomery along one night. The current skater for the Gold was married to another one of Heidi's friends, Angie.

It probably should have been overwhelming—that he'd gone from spending so much time by himself to constantly being with people. But instead of too much, every time he opened up, every time he accepted another person into his life, he felt . . . bigger.

No. More complete. Fulfilled.

Like he was finally fully part of the land of the living instead of alone.

And *that* was fucking incredible.

Even more incredible was that Heidi was just as happy as him. They'd gotten into the habit of mostly staying at her place —frankly, it was nicer, but beyond that, it was also closer to her lab *and* both highways on which they often began their journeys. He didn't mind. He loved her place, loved seeing how proud she was of the life she'd built for herself. So on the weekdays, he'd work until she got off then meet her there, and they'd cook dinner or order in. They'd spend the evening together, watching TV—yes, plenty of her reality shows, but he'd also managed to convince her to watch *Vikings*.

Which she liked for a completely different reason than he did, of course.

He was in for the battles, the politics, the suspense.

She liked all that . . . *and* the male lead.

Though, if he were being completely truthful, when she'd woven "Viking braids" into her hair a few days ago, he'd certainly been able to see the appeal. So much so that they'd spent a very pleasurable evening on the faux fur rug she had in front of her fireplace.

But more than just spending time together, no matter how pleasurable it was, he enjoyed finding all the different ways to take care of her. They could be small, from setting her coffee pot to brew so she'd have it first thing in the morning to taking her trash out, to filling up her car with gas when she'd mentioned it was getting low. Or they could be larger, more time-intensive, like when he'd spent the better part of an afternoon under her kitchen sink because the garbage disposal had gone out.

He understood now that these were all things he'd avoided like the plague when he'd spent the majority of his time traveling—the strings that would tie him more closely to another person, would make him vulnerable, would put him at risk of being hurt if they left or got sick or, God forbid, died.

But he didn't feel scared with Heidi.

Because she was in just as deep.

And because she took care of him in her own way.

He'd found throw pillows on his couch the other day. They were in a "manly" (her words, not his) shade of burgundy that went perfectly with the fuzzy blanket she'd gotten for the foot of his bed. She'd had lunch delivered to his place when she'd known he'd been working on a particularly large project with a deadline looming, had texted him a link for hidden places to visit in California with, "Maybe we can go together?" Then there were all the meals she'd cooked, finding out his favorite foods and incorporating them into the menu, stocking up on a certain brand of popcorn since it was his preferred variety, and how she'd cleared a drawer for him so he could leave some clothes at her place.

In two months' time, he'd gone from feeling unfulfilled and a little lost, to being . . . happy.

Such an inadequate word for all that was in his heart, but it was also the only one that mattered.

Because he was here and *happy*, and not searching for the next adventure that would bring him a slender thread of that elusive fulfillment for just a moment, before that buzz faded and then he was off again, searching for the next thing . . . and the next . . . and the next.

So, yeah, he'd take happy.

Hands down.

"I am sorry about not meeting you," he said, yanking himself out of his head and focusing on the important thing—that being this woman whom he loved to the edge of reason, who loved him back just as completely.

She kissed him lightly on the mouth. "Don't apologize." A wink. "I've been known to get lost in my work every once in a while. You'll just have to owe me." Another wink.

"Is there something in your eye?" he asked innocently.

But she was old hat at his humor by now, so she just reached up and squeezed his cheeks, affecting a baby voice. "Oh, cute little Braddie just thinks he's *so* funny."

"I *know* I'm funny."

"You know what'll be *really* funny?" she asked, dropping her arms and stepping out of the circle of his.

"What?"

"Me leaving you here in your apartment with a rumbling tummy while I go devour the most delicious Mexican food around."

Right on cue, his stomach growled.

"See?" she said, lifting a brow. "Hilarious."

"Not so much." He kissed her, long and sweet and with every bit of affection he possessed for her. "I love you," he murmured when they'd pulled back.

She blinked slightly glazed eyes, the hazel irises deepened to swirls of emerald and russet. Then her lips curved further. "I love you, too. But seriously, I will leave your ass here unless you get it in gear." She pointed toward his closet. "Shoes and jacket on, because it is Friday night, and it's past time for prickly pear margaritas."

"It's going to be a tequila night?"

He'd really enjoyed the last one.

*Really* enjoyed it.

In fact, he'd enjoyed it so much that his legs had been sore enough the following few days to make navigating curbs difficult. And steps. And lifting his foot enough to pull on his pants. And—

Well, it had been damned good.

"Yes, it's going to be a tequila night for me. For you"—she waggled her eyebrows—"only *if* you play your cards right." A beat. "Which means *go get your shoes on*."

It was amazing how quickly people could get dressed when they were motivated.

---

THANKFULLY, the restaurant wasn't far from his apartment, and they managed to sneak into the table just as appetizers were being served.

He pilfered some chips from his brother's plate and hadn't bothered perusing the menu. Instead, he ordered what Heidi did when the server came around to get their meals put in.

Then he stole some more chips from Jaime.

"Hey!"

"Little brother perks," he said chipperly.

Jaime sighed but slid the nachos a little closer. "You're lucky this plate is huge."

"Is that what you said to get Kate to marry you?" he deadpanned.

Heidi giggled, attempting to cover said giggle with her napkin, then gave in, laughing loud enough for everyone at the table to look at her.

"Don't mind me," she said, waving a hand in front of her face, still laughing.

And fuck if that noise didn't fill him up, didn't make him feel like the biggest, baddest motherfucker on the planet. He should be swaggering around this restaurant, showing off his prowess—

Or maybe that should have happened after the last tequila night. Or maybe the Viking one. Or last night. Or—

Suffice to say, he didn't think he'd ever get tired of making love to this woman who'd so easily captured his heart.

"Stop smirking." Jaime socked him in the arm.

Hard.

"Ouch," he muttered, rubbing the injured limb. "What would Mom say?"

Jaime snagged his plate back, smacking Brad's hand when he went to take another chip. "Probably that you deserved it."

He shrugged since that was probably true.

"Speaking of Mom," Jaime said, still guarding his nachos. "They're driving up early. They'll actually be here tomorrow and want to do a family dinner with Kate's family." His eyes flicked past Brad, alighting on Heidi. "That includes you, too," he said, "just in case you'd try to get out of the power of the Moms."

Brad shuddered. His mom and Kate's mom together were a formidable force.

In contrast, Heidi smiled. "I love the Moms."

He groaned. "Pretty soon your mom will join the force, and then there will be *three* Moms."

"Heaven help us," Jaime said.

"My mom would be a scary thought."

He glanced at her, something in the undercurrent of her tone making alarm bells blare. "Why?"

Her eyes did a thing.

Precisely *what* thing was hard to decipher in the low light of the restaurant. He would have said she looked pained, but then it was gone so fast he chalked it up to a shadow, especially because when she spoke again, there was no undercurrent. Just normal Heidi.

"Only that she makes Kate's mom look like a kitten in comparison." She patted his arm. "You'd run away in fear."

"I have to meet her at some point."

Her finger, the nails short and unpolished yet no less feminine, came to her lip, tapped the bottom one. Twice. "But *do* you?"

"I do."

"Damn"—a smile that was completely normal without a weird eye shadow thing and with absolutely no trace of an undercurrent —"and here I was thinking of trying to keep you all to myself."

He glanced around the table, the other occupants unabashedly watching him and Heidi make gooey eyes at each other, then back to his woman. "And that's worked so well."

Another tinkling laugh and she leaned closer, waving a hand in their direction. "Ignore them," she said, pitched loud enough for the table to hear. "They mean nothing."

"I resent that comment." From Cora.

"Meh. I don't need your romance. I've got my own." Courtesy of Kate.

"Well, I, for one, am enjoying the banter. How do those two keep it up?" Via Kels.

"No idea. It's kind of sickening." Added by Stef, who had her casted ankle propped up on a chair.

"*Actually*," Heidi said on a shrug, "it's a gift."

He leaned closer, whispered in her ear. "I thought we were supposed to be ignoring them."

She wrinkled her nose. "Oh. Right."

Except, she didn't say anything.

Probably because, same as him, she'd been having so much fun bantering with him that she couldn't remember what they were supposed to be talking about.

"What were we talking about?" he asked.

Her eyes twinkled, voice dropping to a whisper. "I don't remember."

Chuckling, he thought back, remembered. "Dinner tomorrow," he said. "With the frightening supervillains known as the *Moms*."

Heidi linked her hand with his, stretched up, pressed a kiss to his cheek. "You're just still upset with them because you got in trouble about the wedding cake."

"A man ruins one stupidly expensive cake, and he never hears the end of it," he muttered.

"Rightfully so," Kate chimed in from across the table, drawing them out from each other. "I never even got to eat my lemon layer." She pressed the back of her hand to her forehead, adopted a mournful expression. "Oh, the humanity."

"I *did* say I was sorry," he said, knowing she was joking but still feeling guilty about the entire scenario.

"I'm just teasing." Her face immediately gentled. "It wasn't your fault."

"It was your cock's fault," Heidi said.

And by *said*, he meant practically shouting it across the table . . . right when the restaurant had one of those periodic lulls in conversation . . . which meant that she shouted it across not just the table, but the entire restaurant, too.

Her cheeks flamed as conversations paused, stares turned to her, and then she just shrugged helplessly, setting down the margarita. "Whoops," she whispered. "I guess one margarita goes to your head when you don't eat all day."

"You say that like there's *ever* been a time that one margarita hasn't gone to your head," Kate teased.

"Fair point," she replied.

Brad was more concerned about the fact that, "You haven't eaten all day?"

Heidi winced, patted his shoulder. "Don't get all scowly." Her fingers brushed over his lips. "I was out of muffins, and Molly's was closed by the time we got back yesterday." A shrug. "I meant to stop for lunch, but I forgot. And then I drove to your place when you didn't meet me . . ." Another lift and drop of her shoulders. "The day just ran away from me."

He snagged Jaime's nachos, shoved them in front of her, ignoring his brother's, "Hey!" and ordering her to, "Eat. Now."

She lifted a brow. "Remember what I said about orders?"

He leaned in, whispered into her ear, his cock twitching when she shivered and shifted closer, "You said you only like my orders in bed."

Her head turned, those green-brown eyes coming to his. "I do like them in bed."

Bringing his lips to her ear again, he murmured. "Well, consider that off the table *unless you eat the fucking nachos.*"

For a moment, she melted against him, her shoulder resting against his chest.

Then his words seemed to process, because she straightened, eyes narrowing into a glare. "I ought to kick you out of my bed altogether."

He leaned in, nipped at her bottom lip. "You'd miss me."

"Ouch," she muttered, rubbing the lush curve of her mouth.

"You like it," he countered.

She made a face. "So, what if I do? I still don't have to put up with your—"

He lifted a chip crammed with meat and beans, salsa and sour cream, cheese and guacamole and shoved it into her mouth.

Her glare was back.

But then it softened.

She chewed, swallowed. "I fucking love you, even when you drive me insane."

"I—"

"Love you," Cora interrupted, drawing the focus of the table. "And yadda, yadda, yadda. It's so predictable and lovely, and I'm insanely jealous." She threw her hands up. "Look, I'm happy for you fuckers, but I'm surrounded by gushiness on all sides here! Is it too much for me to ask you to give a single girl some relief around here and not to rub all your HEAs in my face?"

Stef, the only other single girl at the table, nodded. "I second this motion."

Kate opened her mouth, an apology in her expression, but Cora shushed her with a finger in her direction.

"As I said, I am happy for you all. So, no freaking apologies." A beat. "But can we just cool it with the soul-deep declarations? Just through the main course?"

Silence.

Three couples' gazes meeting, guilt drifting between them.

"I said *no guilt!*"

"Well, technically, you said no apologies," Kelsey pointed out.

"Ugh," Cora said.

"Can the soul-deep declarations resume over dessert?" Kate asked innocently.

More silence.

Then "*Ugh!*" Cora and Stef said at the same time.

But then the waiter came and began delivering entrees, and pretty soon the group was overtaken by the latest drama on the episode of *90 Day Fiancé*, and Brad had such a good time hanging out with his woman and her friends—now *his* friends, too—that he forgot all about the thing with Heidi's eyes, the undercurrent in her voice.

Later, he wished he'd remembered.

Wished he'd pushed to get to the bottom of it.

If only he had . . . because so much would have turned out differently.

# TWENTY-FOUR

Heidi

SHE WOKE DELICIOUSLY sore but in the best possible way.

Last night had been the tequila night to end all tequila nights.

She, Kels, Cora, Stef, and Kate had decided to share a pitcher, and thus, it put all other tequila nights to shame.

And it made her look forward to finding other ways to top it, to make *future* tequila nights even better.

She was going to need to start reading erotica in order to up her game.

Brad had given her that hot, sleek smile of his when she'd told him that, kissing her in that long and slow way of his before he'd gotten up to bring her a coffee, and she knew he was looking forward to future tequila nights as much as she was.

He'd brought her a steaming mug—two sugars and a heavy splash of cream—before ordering her to stay in bed.

Probably, she should have protested, should have gotten up and helped him . . . but she was being lazy, and she was tired and cozied up with her back propped up by pillows, her coffee in hand, and he'd offered to cook for her.

So, she was lounging in bed and enjoying his care.

But she was also making a mental note to return that care.

Because he deserved to have this same warm, fuzzy feeling.

In the meantime, she thought, setting her coffee down and burrowing deeper into the blankets, she was going to enjoy the break. Now, if only she didn't need to have her arms out from beneath the comforter to hold her book.

Tough life, she knew.

Sometime later—well, four chapters later—Brad appeared in the doorway, shirtless, with a streak of flour across his chest, a plate laden with goodies in his hands.

"Where's yours?" she asked.

He smiled, crawled into bed next to her, balancing the plate of pancakes, eggs, and bacon in one hand. "Here."

She pressed her lips together.

"So, where's mine?"

Another smile, his body pressing against hers. "Here."

*Ah*, now she saw how this was going to work.

He settled the plate on his lap, scooped up a bite of pancake onto the fork, and lifted it up to her lips.

Right as a knock came on the door.

They both paused.

Then he shrugged. "Ignore it."

Dutifully, she parted her lips, ate the bite he'd offered her.

The knock came again. Trailed by the buzz of her phone.

"This is the continue ignoring part," he said.

Another knock. More buzzing.

He sighed, set the plate on the nightstand. "You get the phone, I'll get the door."

She made a face but dutifully reached for her cell, snagging it from the charging cradle, at the same time her glorious—and still shirtless man—headed to the door.

"Hello?" she asked.

"It's me," Kate's voice came on the line, and it was impossible to miss the panic. "Please, tell me you're staying at Brad's place."

She frowned. "No, we're at mine."

"Shit. Listen, you need to know that your—"

There was a movement in the doorway, drawing her gaze up, and . . . horror dawned.

"—mom is in town."

Her cell dropped to the mattress.

---

FIFTEEN MINUTES LATER, she and Brad were both fully dressed, her phone was back in the charging stand, and she was seated at the kitchen table while Brad redistributed the contents of the two-for-one plate into . . . well, two plates, and then made up one more.

For her mother.

Who was wiping a finger across the wooden surface of Heidi's table.

Colleen grimaced and reached into the handbag she hadn't yet put down, extracting a package of wet wipes then cleaning the area in front of her.

Then the back of the chair, and the seat, *and* the fork and knife Brad had placed on a napkin for her before serving up breakfast.

Brad, who'd turned from the counter, two plates in hand, was watching the exercise with raised brows. Brows he then turned onto her.

And all she could do was shrug helplessly.

This was her mother.

The *lite* version of her mother.

Because more . . . of her mother's motherness would come.

"I believe I bought you placemats, dear," she said.

Ugly ass ones with puke green flowers and red trim—like the most unattractive version of Christmas someone could imagine.

"Ah, yes." She cleared her throat. "I only use them for very special occasions." Brad set a plate in front of her mom, rounded the table to set one in front of Heidi, pressing a kiss to the side of her neck.

She smiled up at him. "Thanks," she murmured.

He brushed his fingers over her cheek. "You're welcome."

Then he returned for his own and sat down next to her.

Heidi didn't bother saying anything. Her mother wouldn't trouble herself to listen to anything she had to say that wasn't what she wanted to hear, so the best tactic was to wait for her to start the conversation.

"Breakfast this late in the day?"

Ah.

Cool.

She was going to start off with a bang.

"Yup," Heidi said, feeling Brad's gaze on her face. She glanced at him out of the corner of her eye, saw his features drawn in confusion.

He cleared his throat. "Heidi and I had a late night."

"Hmm."

"And I have to say I'm a big fan of breakfast, no matter the time of day," he added.

"I see."

Except, she answered it like she always said something that wasn't what she wanted to hear. Like someone was suggesting they go out and slaughter unicorns.

Heidi continued to ignore her, glancing at Brad as she shoveled in food. "Thank you," she said between bites. "This is delicious."

He rested his palm on her thigh. "You're welcome."

"*You* cooked?"

His gaze went from Heidi to her mother. "Heidi has been working really hard," he said. "I figured she could use a break."

A sniff. "Working."

More unicorn slaughtering.

And she knew that she had to take this in hand. "Yes, Mom, working. I'm still at the lab, and I love it."

"And does *Brad* love it?"

Her throat seized, but before she could summon a reply, he answered, "I enjoy spending whatever time with her I can, and yes, I love that she has a job that fulfills her."

Stink face.

That was the only way she could think to describe her mother's expression.

"Mom—" she began.

"What do you do?"

Brad was nonplussed by the sharp question. "I'm a web designer."

"And can you make a living at that?"

He chuckled. "I've been making a living at it for close to ten years now."

"Ah."

Cue silence.

"Why'd you decide to come into town, Mom?" she asked into that tense quiet.

"Your father had a conference."

And neither of them had decided to tell her. Right. Her dad, she could understand. Keeping track of a schedule wasn't his strong suit. But her mother . . . she was organized, she knew what was coming.

She just expected Heidi to always drop everything and be available.

"Oh, that's great," Brad said. "I'd love to meet him. Are you two free later? My family is in town, and we're having a big dinner with my brother's wife's family. Actually, I'm sure you guys probably already know Kate's parents, huh?" He glanced at Heidi. "Since you guys have known each other since college."

Heidi shrugged. Yes, her parents *had* met Kate's. And it had gone . . . well, about as well as a nuclear explosion. Kate's parents were . . . nice. Which wasn't a fair assessment to her dad, she knew. He was a decent person, if not a bit detached from anything that wasn't the science in his brain.

It was just that her mom was . . . her mom.

"Actually," she began.

Meanwhile, Brad was still talking. "It's always a good time, and I'm sure they'd love to have you—"

Her mother daintily picked up a fork, cut off a truly minis-cule bite of pancake, and ate it. Then shuddered.

For fuck's sake.

"—if you're available and—"

"I'm sure they're busy," Heidi blurted. "My father's confer-ence schedule is always hectic, and he's usually tired after—"

"Kate McLeod?"

Brad smiled. "She's a Huntington, now, but yes, she was a McLeod."

Her mom's eyes widened, hunger inside them. The very same hangers-on hunger she'd had the first time she'd met Kate's parents. The same hunger that had Heidi promising herself she would never, ever bring their two families into contact again.

"They're busy," she said quickly.

"Actually," her mom said. "No, we're not. We'd love to come."

She tried another way. "It's impolite to add guests—"

"It's fine, sweetheart," he said. "My mom is always happy to welcome more, and I know Kate's mom feels the same."

Because, of course, they did.

Because the Moms were both wonderful.

Unlike hers.

"Great," her mother said. "Then it's settled. Your father and I will join in on the dinner."

## TWENTY-FIVE

Brad

HE'D FUCKED UP.

He'd realized that after Heidi's mom, Colleen, had left to "go get ready" and he'd finally seen Heidi's face.

He'd known it when her parents had shown up in the rental car, her dad in jeans and a polo that would fit right in with the Huntingtons and McLeods, and her mother in a cocktail dress.

With pearls.

She looked beautiful.

She just didn't look like she was ready to go to a casual family-style dinner.

Fancy eight-course meal? Yes.

BBQ chicken on paper plates? No.

But he hadn't realized *exactly* how much he'd fucked up until dinner.

When Colleen had latched onto Kate's mom, Marabelle, like a limpet, asking her all about her cosmetic business and how much money she'd made and then approaching practically every item in the large ranch-style house and expounding on how expensive the built-in cabinet must be, and—oh look—that TV was huge, it must be super pricey, and what about the outdoor kitchen? That surely must have cost an arm and leg, especially with that glass tile backsplash.

It wasn't so much that she was complimenting Marabelle's style choices . . . it was just . . . all so insincere.

Over the top.

Disingenuous.

But that still wasn't the moment when he'd realized the extent of his fucked-up-ness.

Nope.

That came from the way she'd treated Heidi.

The way she was *still* treating Heidi. And look, his own mom had taught him to treat people with kindness and respect, but she'd also taught him to stand up to bullies.

Colleen was a bully.

He didn't know *why* she was a bully, but he just knew that she must have been that way for a long time, long enough that Frank, her scientist husband, and Heidi hardly seemed to notice the barely veiled barbs, the disapproving looks.

But as the wine flowed and the dinner went on, the barbs became more obvious.

And the hold on his temper grew decidedly tenuous.

"Tell me what you're working on in your lab," Marabelle said. Then chuckled. "Well, tell me whatever you can that's not top secret, that is." She glanced over at Colleen. "Isn't it amazing that your daughter runs her own lab? I heard her last paper was peer reviewed in *The Journal*."

For the first time, he saw Frank perk up, lifting his head from his plate of chocolate cake and reaching across the table to pat his daughter's hand. "It was a fantastic article."

"But she's still over thirty and unmarried."

All eyes at the table turned to Colleen.

Then went back to Heidi—who was gorgeous in an emerald blouse, loose-fitting jeans, and minimal makeup that didn't hide the red stain on her cheeks. "Lucky for me, there's more to life than wedding bells." She smiled at Kate. "No offense to my newly-married friends."

Kate smiled sympathetically. "None taken. God knows, I spent plenty of time being over thirty and unmarried."

"Except—"

"Enough, Mom," Heidi said.

Colleen's jaw tightened. "Well, even if you don't care enough to give me grandchildren, the least you could do is go easy on the sugar and carbs so you can fit into a nice wedding dress." She sniffed. "That is, if you can even get Brad down the aisle."

Kate gasped.

Heidi's eyes slid closed.

And he lost it.

He slammed his hands on the table as he shot to his feet, his chair tipping over backward and hitting the floor with a loud *thwack*. "Where in the hell do you get off treating your daughter that way?"

Primly, she turned in his direction. "E*xcuse* me?" she asked archly.

"No, you're not excused," he snapped. "Your behavior is atrocious. Your daughter is the most wonderful woman I have ever met, and I'm lucky enough to love her. And yet you treat her like she's not worthy." He slammed his hands on the table again, making several people jump. "You don't fucking deserve to breathe her air."

"How dare—"

"How dare *I*?" He stepped back from the table, straightened his chair. "Is that what you were going to say? How dare I stick up for your daughter? How dare I love her? How dare I be so fucking proud of her for doing something she is incredible at, something she enjoys?"

"I don't care if she plays at the lab," Collen said with a sniff. "She still doesn't have the important things. Plus, she hardly ever sees us."

"I wonder why," he growled. "With a mother like you, it's a wonder she even let you walk through her door this morning. Oh wait, *I* was the one who let you in." A beat as gasps surrounded the table. "Your daughter likely would have used that big juicy brain of hers to slam the door in your face—"

"That's enough."

His own mother's voice was probably the only thing that could have stopped him in that instance.

He glanced over at her, vision tinged red with fury.

She cupped his cheek. "Honey, that's enough."

Forcing himself to take a deep breath, he nodded, sat back down.

"What manners," Colleen huffed.

"Colleen—" Frank warned.

She ignored him, her chin lifting somewhere in the level of the atmosphere. "I've never had anyone speak to me in such a way," she said. "Maybe I don't want such a man to date my daughter."

"Enough, Mom," Heidi said. "That's—"

"The rudeness is just . . . inexplicable. I've never said a cross word to anyone and—"

A muscle in his mom's jaw twitched, but she merely glanced over at Marabelle.

Who nodded.

"I think it's time to leave," his mom said.

"Yes"—Colleen placed her napkin on the table—"it's getting late. This dinner should have ended long ago—"

"No," Marabelle said, standing up and striding into the hall, where she opened the front door. "What I mean is that *you* should go, and the rest of us will enjoy our evening."

Colleen froze in the middle of collecting her purse. "Excuse me?"

"You heard me fine," Marabelle said. "I won't tell you not to come back because I'm not the kind of person who closes doors on other people. Hence, the reason you're back here in my house, despite the rudeness you showed the last time you visited." She crossed her arms. "However, I will tell you that as of this moment, you certainly will not be welcomed back in this house unless you're prepared to treat everyone with respect and understanding, including your lovely, wonderful daughter."

Heidi blinked rapidly, her gaze falling to the table. "Mom," she said. "Please, just go." Brad took her hand. She pulled away, held them tightly in her lap.

"Well, I never—"

Frank seemed to finally grow a pair. "Colleen," he snapped. "That is *more* than enough."

She whirled on him, glaring darkly. "Don't you dare—"

He stood abruptly, his chair screeching against the floor. "Don't you see that you're embarrassing yourself? That you're embarrassing your daughter?" His shoulders straightened. "And me. You're embarrassing me." A beat, his eyes, so similar to Heidi's skimmed the table. "You need to apologize. To everyone."

Colleen crossed her arms and glared at the ceiling.

Frank sighed, pushed in the chair, and kissed Heidi—whose expression had turned bleak, her eyes reddened, her skin dull and pale—on the cheek. "*My* apologies for my wife's inexcusable rudeness," he said to the table and grabbed their two jackets from the hook, draping them over one arm, before his eyes went to Marabelle's. "I hope that if we are ever given the honor of an invitation to your wonderful home again that my wife will find her manners. Either that, or you can feel free to leave her off the invite."

Colleen bristled. "How—"

"I," he said, speaking loud enough to drown out Colleen, "on the other hand, cannot thank you enough for the care you've shown my daughter." His gaze went to Heidi, who had dropped her eyes to her folded hands. "Thank you for giving that to her." His voice dropped. "She deserves it and so much more. She deserves all the happiness in the world." A squeeze to her shoulder before he cleared his throat, his volume increasing, forced cheerfulness in his tone. "We'll let you folks get on with your night. I'm sure you'll have a much better time without us."

With that, he snagged Colleen's arm and dragged the still-sputtering woman out the front door.

A heartbeat later, Marabelle slammed it behind them.

Then locked it, rubbing her hands together.

"I meant it when I said I don't normally close doors on people." She rolled her head from side to side. "But damn, did that feel good."

She laughed, and the room joined in.

But not the *whole* room. Because his ears prickled, realizing that someone's laugh had been missing.

Not someone's.

Heidi's.

Because she was gone.

# TWENTY-SIX

Heidi

SHE WAS HIDING in the darkened shadows of Kate's parent's back yard and wondering if she could dig a hole deep enough to hide in when Brad found her.

Hands around her waist, a firm chest at her spine.

Just holding her silently for long moments.

"I'm sorry," she whispered when she could speak without sobbing.

"For what?"

A startled laugh as she spun in his arms. "For what?" she asked. "For *what?*" She shook her head. "She was being awful, doing the same stuff she always does, and I couldn't break that fucking cycle. I just sat there like a fucking lump, taking it." She pushed away from him then stalked away. "I just let her treat me like shit."

"First," he said, coming up behind her and snagging her hand. "It was damned hard trying to get a word in edgewise with the woman." He tugged her toward him. "Second, sometimes it's not the easiest telling people you love that they're out of line." He smoothed back her hair. "Third, I repeat, there was not a lot of room in that conversation for more words, even though I do seem to remember you telling her to stop."

"She didn't listen, though, did she?"

"Does she listen to anyone?"

He had a point there.

"No." But . . . *God* she was so fucking embarrassed. That scene was just one of those special moments her mother excelled at creating and then adding in the rest of her behavior. It was right up there with the nuclear explosion of her parents' first meeting with Kate's mom and dad.

Only this time, she'd managed to squeeze out a few more words.

Barely.

"Baby," he whispered. "No one is upset at you."

She knew that—well, she *supposed* she knew that, but . . . how could they *not* be mad at her? It was her mom that had ruined the fun night, her mom who'd said all the rude things. It was absolutely despicable, the way her mother had acted.

"I had to battle Kate and both of our mothers for the privilege to make sure you're okay."

She winced. "They should just get on with their meal."

"*We* should get on with our dessert before my dad gorges himself on the rest of the chocolate cake." She smiled, thinking it had definitely been gorge-worthy, or at least the one bite of it she'd managed to eat had been absolutely delicious before her mom had gone on her tear. "Plus, when everyone is done, we're going to play *Ticket to Ride*." He laughed. "And I should warn you, *my* mom has been practicing since Marabelle destroyed her so incredibly badly last time."

Somehow, despite the scene in the dining room, this man still made her laugh.

"There it is," he whispered.

"There's what?"

"The laugh that makes my heart fill with joy." He cupped the side of her neck, drew her against him once again. "Baby, no one cares that your mom is the worst, and certainly not *the* Moms. They've decided to make you an official Huntington-McLeod adopted daughter, and their pledge is to ensure that you understand you're, quote 'beautiful, smart, and beyond wonderful'—all of which are true, by the way." His thumb brushed across her cheek, and she realized she was crying. "I'd also add strong, sexy as shit with Viking braids, and so fucking funny that you give my banter skills a run for the money."

"Brad," she whispered.

"So, good luck dealing with the pair of them," he said. "In fact, I heard Marabelle plotting with my mom that they were going to wrap you up in so much love you would never be able to escape."

She sighed. "They really are quite wonderful."

"You say that now," he teased, then loosened his hold, lacing their fingers together and drawing her toward the house. "Come on, let's go cheat by working together so neither of our moms can get the most successful railroad."

"Wait."

He stopped. "What, baby?"

"Are you sure no one is mad?" Her teeth found her bottom lip, nibbled lightly. "I ruined their night and—"

He kissed her gently and filled with so much love and tender affection that she felt her heart melt. "I can absolutely promise you that no one is mad." He paused. "Well, no one currently allowed in Marabelle's house. *Your* mom on the other hand . . ."

She tugged her hand free, covered her face, groaning. "I hate that I didn't stand up for myself."

He came close again, rubbed his hand up and down her

back. "You know what the great part about being in a relationship is?"

Her shoulders relaxed the slightest bit. "Besides the copious amount of orgasms?"

A smile. "Yes, besides those."

"I don't know," she said. "What?"

"That you don't have to fight all of your battles alone."

"Look at you, sounding all logical." She wrinkled her nose. "Of course, I know you're right, and I do thank you for standing up for me. Knowing that you'd go to bat for me, even in an uncomfortable situation . . . it makes me feel all warm and fuzzy inside."

"Does that mean you love me even more?"

She made a face. "Not that your ego needs it, but yes. You saying those things, sticking up for me . . . yes, I love you even more."

The breeze picked up, rustling through her hair, making her shiver.

"You're cold." He bundled her against his warm chest, wrapping his arms tightly around her. "Let's go inside."

She let him lead her toward the house. "I just wish I could have said . . ." She trailed off, realization finally dawning on her, making her go still in his arms, her brain putting the puzzle pieces together.

"What, baby?" he prompted.

"It wouldn't have mattered what I said, would it?"

He just stroked a hand down her spine, let her continue to think about that. After a moment, she shook her head. "No," she murmured. "I don't think it would have."

Brad loved her. He had her back. And further that, her dad, who normally was so deep in his own head had recognized she needed that, too, needed someone to build her up rather than tear her down. She supposed that her mom also loved her, at least in some unhealthy way, a way that made it so she would never turn down an opportunity to make Heidi feel small.

But that didn't have anything to do with her.

Did that suck?

Hell yeah.

Did that make a part of her feel like shit?

Hell fucking yeah.

But could she truly do anything to change her mother's behavior? No.

Nothing she did would ever make her mom change. So, she could only alter *her* reaction, adjust *her* expectations. Heidi could work on extracting herself from the situations, make sure she didn't allow herself to be waylaid into scenarios she didn't want to participate in. She could keep her distance from her mom, only allow the interactions *she* was comfortable with.

And . . . she could continue surrounding herself with people who loved her for who she was.

Who didn't see her as a failure.

Who instead saw her flaws and loved her all the more for them.

"Heidi."

She stopped and stared up at him. "I love you."

His face softened. "I love you." Fingers on her cheek. "I'll love you until—"

"Come on already!" Jaime shouted from the door. "Just kiss her until she gets all dopey and forgets what happened. Then we'll convince her we don't care what happened—"

"Unless, of course, she beats me in *Ticket to Ride*," Marabelle called. "Then all bets are off!"

Heidi had frozen at the sound of Jaime's voice.

The addition of Marabelle's made her smile.

Brad smoothed back her hair. "I guess I'd better listen to him."

"Wh—?"

But she didn't get to finish the question because his lips were on hers, and then he was kissing her until she was loopy, until her heart pounded and her pulse was skittering through her veins.

Then he took her inside to play a board game.

As though it were a normal night and not one where her heart had seemed to grow three sizes.

"Hey," Jaime said as they started to walk past him.

She glanced up, but he was looking at Brad, smiling in that paternalistic, older brother way he just exuded.

"For the record, Mom just told me she's not going to worry about you anymore."

Brad went still, *so* still.

Then his body relaxed, a long sigh escaping him, and he clapped Jaime on the shoulder. "Love you, bro."

"Love you, too." Jaime nodded, and after Kate popped her head into the hall, he hustled into the dining room.

"What was that about?" Heidi whispered as they followed him.

He slowed down, tugging her to a halt with him. "That—"

"Ticket to *Ride!*" Marabelle called from the dining room.

His lips curved up into that special, slow, sexy smile that he reserved only for her.

"I'll tell you—"

"Now!"

Lips on hers for the briefest moment. "Some other time."

Heidi's heart grew another size. "Sometime in our long, happy future together?"

Another smile—this one hot, tinged with sweet. "Yes."

Marabelle's head poked in through the opening. "Ticket—"

"To ride!" they finished in unison.

And then they went into the kitchen. To finally play that board game.

On a night that felt extraordinary, but would become commonplace as the years went by, her heart growing and growing until it seemed to take up all the space in her body.

But that wasn't scary any longer. All the love she felt for them made her stronger, instead of weaker, built her up instead of tore her down.

Because she had her family—the one she'd made, the one she'd chosen.

And she had this man.

Who'd turned normal into extraordinary.

# EPILOGUE

Brad, six months later

PINK-PAINTED nails digging into pale white sand.

A lusciously curved body curled up next to his.

A paperback propped on his chest as she read her latest historical romance.

It was funny, but in all his travels, he had never been one for sitting on a beach all day, having cocktails delivered at his elbow, the hot sun shining down through an umbrella overhead.

But with Heidi at his side like this, he was hard-pressed to picture another type of vacation.

Of course, it might also be the sex.

He could now say with complete authority that he didn't mind getting sand into all sorts of crevices when it meant that he could be with this woman.

Tomorrow they would be going back home to the Bay Area, to Heidi's condo with his newly finished—and exceptionally organized thanks to his woman—office, and they'd be heading back to reality.

Except, reality was . . . heaven.

So they might be leaving the gorgeous beach and warm sand. They wouldn't have cocktails delivered to their cabana, left at their sides by friendly attendants. They'd be back in the fog, in the traffic, in the long hours at the lab and long hours behind a computer.

But they'd also be going back to movie nights and popcorn, to coffee while cuddled up in bed, and blustery trips to the beach.

They'd be going back to the life they'd built.

The huge, wonderful, amazing life they'd built.

Only . . . Heidi didn't know it, but she would be going back with one additional souvenir.

The diamond ring currently taking up space in his pocket because he hadn't been able to let it out of his sight.

He had it planned for dinner. He'd made all the arrangements, a moonlight stroll on the beach, a private dinner at a table perched just above the waves. They'd have the stars and the moon, and then he'd get down on one knee and—

"I was thinking."

Blinking, he glanced down at her, at the woman who held his heart in the palm of her hand, who was so fucking strong and smart and beautiful, and smiled. "About what?"

She set her book down, shifted so she could rest her chin on her folded arms that sat on his chest. Then she smiled.

And damn if his heart still didn't skip a beat.

"Uh-oh," he teased. "That's a very calculating look. What am I about to get myself into?"

A splash of pink on her cheeks. "I was thinking."

He smirked. "You said that already. Thinking about what?"

"Well, our flight home connects through Vegas," she said. "So, I thought we could extend our trip for one more day and . . "

"Go gambling?"

She sighed, narrowed her eyes at him. "Brad," she warned.

"What?" he asked innocently.

She huffed. "We could do the most Vegas-y thing ever and take a page out of Kels and Tanner's book—"

*And* then he decided to forget the dinner, forget the moonlight and crashing waves and proposal under the stars. Placing a finger over her lips, he used his other hand to reach into his pocket.

He didn't skip the one knee—which required him to do a fair amount of maneuvering, he had to admit—but then she was sitting up and he was on one knee, and he had the ring box open.

"Heidi, my love, my heart, my everything—"

"Yes!"

Laughter bubbled up in his chest. "I haven't even asked you yet."

"You don't have to." She launched herself into his arms, making him fumble to grab her, hold on to the ring, and not end up on his ass. He was only successful in two of the three, but since they were the most important two, he didn't mind the sand getting up his swim trunks. Especially when she said, "The answer to any question you ask me will always be yes."

"*Any?*" he asked, tugging at a strand of her hair. "Are you sure you want to commit to that?"

A glare. "Stop teasing and kiss me."

"In a minute," he said, then looked deeply into those beautiful hazel eyes and asked her the most important question of his life. "Heidi Greene, will you marry me?"

Her expression gentled. "Yes, baby. I will." A beat, her lips curving. "Now, will you kiss me already?"

He smiled, cupped her cheek. "One more thing first."

A mock-annoyed huff.

Then a smile when he slipped the ring on her finger.

And *then* he kissed her.

"So, Vegas?" she asked when they broke for air, breath coming in rapid bursts. "Want to hit up a chapel with me?"

He wanted nothing more.

But . . . "Don't you want to have a big wedding with the giant dress and the bridesmaids and the hundreds of guests?"

She shuddered. "No. I just want you."

"What about your friends?" he asked, wanting to marry her more than anything but also wanting to make sure she had everything she had ever dreamed of. "Don't you want them to be part of your wedding?"

Fingers on his jaw, her mouth very close to his. "Honey," she said. "I never fantasized about having a big wedding with the white, puffy dress and the bouquet and the multi-tiered wedding cake"—a smile he could practically taste, her lips were so near—"that can be knocked over by an errant groomsman—"

"It was the Fuzz."

A brush of her mouth across his. "Sure, it was." Another. "But cocks aside"—she grinned, and he snorted—"what I'm trying to tell you is that all I've ever dreamed of is finding a person who loves me for who I am, someone who I'm not afraid to let close because they would see my flaws and understand that they are just another piece of me to appreciate." She straightened, her eyes growing damp. "And *you're* that person. You're the one who's made me see that I was worthy of all that . . . and so much more. You're the one who gave me more than I could ever imagine, so"—she cupped his jaw—"know that I love you, honey, and I want to marry you so fucking much. In fact, the only thing I want to do slightly more is to make babies with you."

His heart, fuck, it squeezed tight, so much emotion coiling in his stomach that it took his breath away.

"You want babies?"

She nodded.

*Thud-thud.*

*Thud-thud.*

*Thud-thud.*

He stood, tugging her to her feet.

"What's the matter?" she asked as he started dragging her across the sand. "Brad!"

He turned back, swept her into his arms. "We need to get started."

"Packing?"

A slow shake of his head. "No, sweetheart. On the babies."

She laughed, wrapped her arms around him. "That sounds like the best idea you've ever had."

He waggled his brows. "The best—"

She kissed him.

Then he got to work on that best idea.

# EPILOGUE

## PART TWO

Stef

## SHE LOVED SAN FRANCISCO.

She loved her friends—well the ones she'd made in the last six months, not the jerkwads who'd all but abandoned her after she and Jeremy had broken up.

What she *didn't* love?

The lack of sex in her life.

Sure, she had her drawer of friendly vibrators, but . . . it wasn't the same.

Okay, sometimes it *was* better.

But oftentimes it was . . . well, a bit lacking. She wanted a hot, hard, strong body poised on top of her. She wanted a man to pick her up and pin her to a wall, pounding deep and hard and—

*Hard.*

The trouble was that there weren't a lot of men who were interested in a frumpy scientist who had an obsession with *Stargate.*

Which was why she was lying in bed wearing her favorite cozy pajamas and trying to work up the urge to . . . swipe right.

Because the man on the app was gorgeous.

When she'd first seen him, her vagina had jumped up, doing a happy dance—complete with pasties and sparklers and a skimpy thong. Well, not so much skimpy because skimpy and her body type didn't mix, but she'd at least slip into some high-cut bikini bottoms, and she'd *definitely* shave her legs.

"Just do it," she whispered.

But the problem with swiping right was that this beautiful man with the sexiest smile she'd ever laid eyes on would invariably swipe left on her picture, and she'd still be here, lying in bed, in her pajamas, and reaching for her vibrator instead of the man himself.

Le sigh.

"No," she muttered. "No men."

She tossed her phone on the mattress, hit play on her show, and settled in with her glass of wine and her sexy, just as fictional as the man in the app, Colonel Jack O'Neill.

See?

Her life was full.

She had good friends. She had good vibrators. She had a good job.

She had a *great* dog.

"I don't need anything else, do I, Fred?"

Her fluffy friend, with his adorable golden retriever face and his fuzzy tail, glanced up at her. He was exhausted after a long day of hiking and currently curled up in the space where her imaginary man might reside.

Another *see*?

Because she didn't have room for the app man, any more than she had room for that fictional colonel.

It was her and Fred and her bottle of wine.

That was good enough.

Except . . . it wasn't good enough when she finished that wine, and her mind got thinking, and her reserve disappeared into the wind.

It wasn't good enough when she used her slightly drunk coordination to pick up her cell, and her slightly drunk lack of inhibition to . . . swipe right.

Bleary eyes shutting, she let her arm drop to the bed, the phone slipping out of her grip, sleep claiming her fast and heavily.

And in the morning? When she'd almost forgotten about the fictional man and her drunk swiping . . .

Well, in the morning, she woke up and saw—

He'd swiped right, too.

Oh, fuck.

—Bad Swipe, coming June 28th, 2021

# BAD SWIPE

Read Stef's story, coming June 28th, 2021.
Preorder your copy at www.books2read.com/badswipe

## BILLIONAIRE'S CLUB

Bad Night Stand

Bad Breakup

Bad Husband

Bad Hookup

Bad Divorce

Bad Fiancé

Bad Boyfriend

Bad Blind Date

Bad Wedding

Bad Engagement

Bad Bridesmaid

Bad Swipe

## ALSO BY ELISE FABER

*Billionaire's Club* (**all stand alone**)

Bad Night Stand

Bad Breakup

Bad Husband

Bad Hookup

Bad Divorce

Bad Fiancé

Bad Boyfriend

Bad Blind Date

Bad Wedding

Bad Engagement

Bad Bridesmaid

Bad Swipe

*Gold Hockey* (**all stand alone**)

Blocked

Backhand

Boarding

Benched

Breakaway

Breakout

Checked

Coasting

Centered

Charging

Caged (April 12th, 2021)

**_Breakers Hockey_ (all stand alone)**

Broken (May 24th, 2021)

**_Love, Action, Camera (all stand alone)_**

Dotted Line

Action Shot

Close-Up

End Scene

Meet Cute (April 5th, 2021)

**_Love After Midnight_ (all stand alone)**

Rum And Notes

Virgin Daiquiri

On The Rocks

Sex On The Seats (April 26th, 2021)

**_Life Sucks Series_ (all stand alone)**

Train Wreck

Hot Mess

Dumpster Fire

Clusterf*@k (August 16th, 2021)

**_Roosevelt Ranch Series_ (all stand alone, series complete)**

Disaster at Roosevelt Ranch

Heartbreak at Roosevelt Ranch

Collision at Roosevelt Ranch

Regret at Roosevelt Ranch

Desire at Roosevelt Ranch

## *Phoenix Series* (read in order)

Phoenix Rising

Dark Phoenix

Phoenix Freed

## *Phoenix: LexTal Chronicles* (rereleasing soon, stand alone, Phoenix world)

From Ashes

In Flames

To Smoke (October 18th, 2021)

## *KTS Series*

Fire and Ice (Hurt Anthology, stand alone)

Riding The Edge

Crossing The Line (March 22nd, 2021)

Leveling The Field (June 14th, 2021)

## *Stand Alones*

Someday, Maybe (YA)

# ABOUT THE AUTHOR

*USA Today* bestselling author, Elise Faber, loves chocolate, Star Wars, Harry Potter, and hockey (the order depending on the day and how well her team -- the Sharks! -- are playing). She and her husband also play as much hockey as they can squeeze into their schedules, so much so that their typical date night is spent on the ice. Elise changes her hair color more often than some people change their socks, loves sparkly things, and is the mom to two exuberant boys. She lives in Northern California. Connect with her in her Facebook group, the Fabinators or find more information about her books at www.elisefaber.com.

facebook.com/elisefaberauthor

amazon.com/author/elisefaber

bookbub.com/profile/elise-faber

instagram.com/elisefaber

goodreads.com/elisefaber

pinterest.com/elisefaberwrite

www.ingramcontent.com/pod-product-compliance
Lightning Source LLC
Chambersburg PA
CBHW022113240626
47153CB00007B/2349